BLACK FROST

BOOK 2

CRAIG HALLORAN

Dragon Wars: Black Frost – Book 2

By Craig Halloran

★ ★ ★ ★

Copyright © 2019 by Craig Halloran

Amazon Edition

TWO-TEN BOOK PRESS

PO Box 4215, Charleston, WV 25364

ISBN eBook: 978-1-946218-68-1

ISBN paperback: 978-1-654612-20-7

ISBN Hardback: 978-1-946218-69-8

www.craighalloran.com

Publisher's Note

This book is a work of fiction. Names, characters, places, and incidents either are the product of the author's imagination or are used fictitiously, and any resemblance to actual persons, living or dead, events, or locales is entirely coincidental.

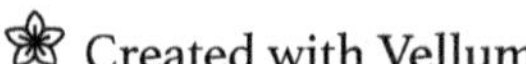 Created with Vellum

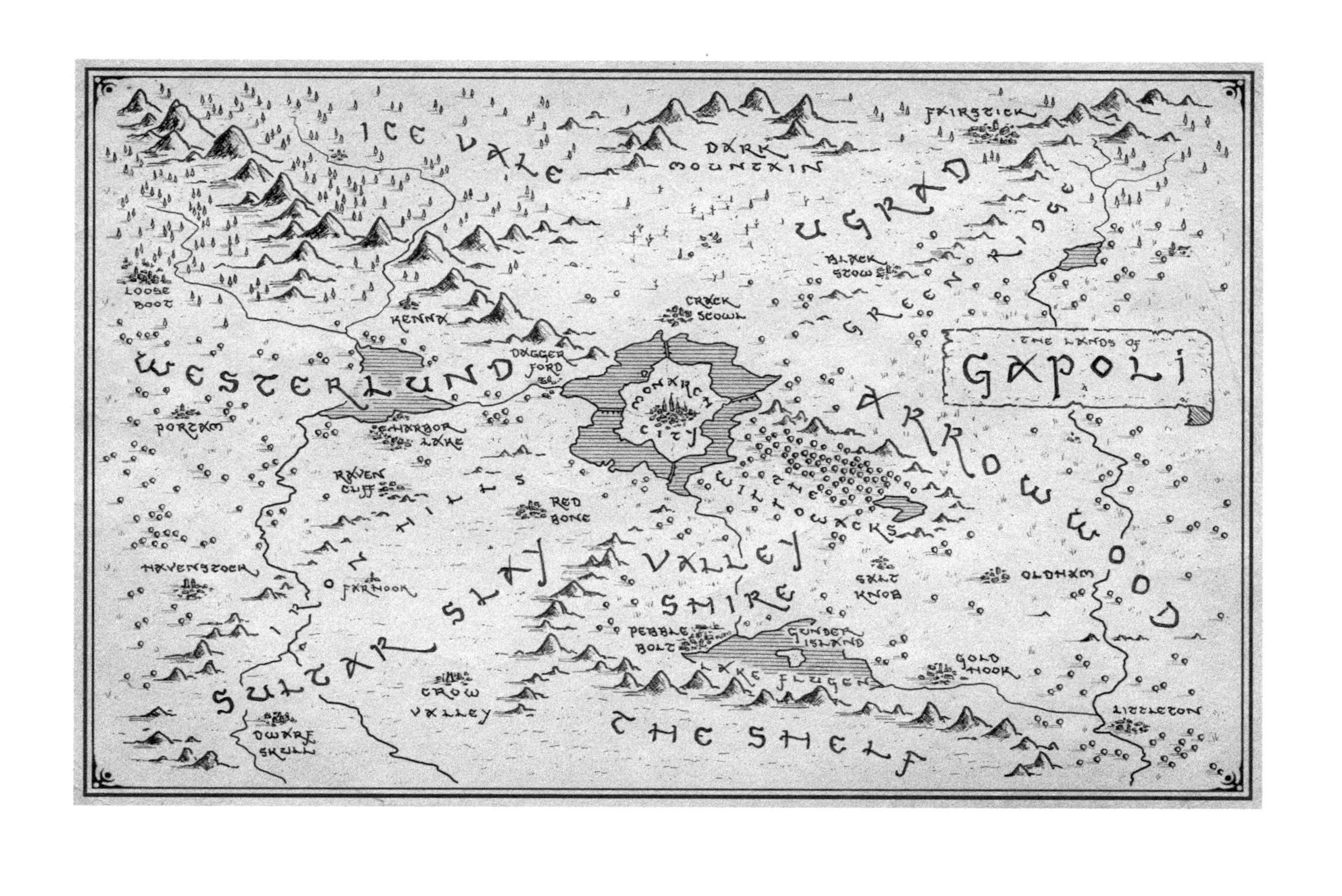

THE LANDS OF
GAPOLI
ICE VALE
DARK MOUNTAIN
FAIRSTICK
UGRAD
GREEN RIDGE
BLACK STONE
LOOSE BOOT
KENNA
CRACK SCOWL
WESTERLUND
DAGGER FORD
MONARCH CITY
PORTAM
E HARBOR LAKE
RAVEN CLIFF
IRON HILLS
RED BONE
ARROWWOOD
WILTTEWACKS
HAVENSTOCK
FARNOOK
SULTAR SLAT
VALLEY
SHIRE
SALT KNOB
BONY
OLDHAM
PEBBLE BOLT
GUNDER ISLAND
GOLD HOOK
CROW VALLEY
LAKE FLUGEN
DWARF SKULL
THE SHELF
LITTLETON

IRON HILLS

In less than a month, Grey Cloak's life had been turned upside down and inside out. He, a stripling elf, and his human blood brother, Dyphestive, had left the laborious sanctuary of Havenstock to seek out greener pastures. Since their departure, they'd been robbed, beaten, and jailed. Then they'd joined a group called Talon, a band of adventurers, seeking a fortune and wisdom. They'd fought the undead and faced dragons. But that glorious road had come to a dead end in the rocky forest terrain of the Iron Hills. A horde of bloodthirsty goblins had chased them over a league and finally hemmed them in at the mouth of a shallow cave.

Grey Cloak smirked as he faced the throng of ugly fiends. He was standing behind Talon's leaders, the wizard Dalsay and the monarch knight Adanadel, who were both human. The only thing between the company and the goblin horde was a black figurine that Dalsay had set on the ground seconds earlier. Inky-black and milky-gray smoke slowly spewed out of the figurine as if it were a chimney. Inside the billowing cloud, a form began to take shape.

The hairs on the nape of Grey Cloak's neck stood on end. He spun his sword and dagger end over end, his heart in his throat.

Dyphestive was standing beside Grey Cloak, panting, sweat glistening on his broad face and dripping off of his chin. He was gripping the iron sword in two white-knuckled hands.

Browning, a rugged man in chain mail, was brandishing a broadsword and buckler, eyes growing by the second. He gulped in mouthfuls of air.

Zora the half-elf brushed against Grey Cloak's shoulder. Two steel daggers filled her hands. She swallowed and took a deep breath.

Eyeing the smoke, Tanlin, a human rogue, quietly mumbled, "Not again. Not again."

The beautiful elven mystic Tatiana was holding an amulet that burned like fire in her hand. Her eyes were locked on the growing cloud pillar, and she was mumbling softly.

A few dozen yards away, one of the two goblin chieftains stepped forward. The huge greasy fiend, decorated in bone jewelry and metal piercings, glowered at the smoke pillar with one watery eye. He was carrying a war hammer as long as a shovel and swung it over his shoulder. He eyed the smoke and Dalsay and said, "You think your magic can stop my tribe? Me, my brothers? Hah! We shall slaughter your dark forces with superior numbers!" He raised his war hammer high in the air and waved it around. "What do you say, my brothers?"

The goblins let out deafening bellows. Their war hounds barked and howled like demons.

The figure inside the smoke started to solidify into a more distinct shape.

"May the dragon's blessing be with us," Tatiana whispered. The leaves rustled, and the wind began to take the smoke away. She gasped.

Browning, Dalsay, and Adanadel stepped back, and the cajoling goblins fell silent. Grey Cloak's heart skipped as he gazed upon a man the likes of which he'd never imagined before.

Staring down the members of Talon was a muscle-bound warrior seated on a horse-sized two-headed dog and wearing a full spiked helmet fashioned from dark metal. Blue eyes blazed like fire behind two rectangular eyelets with hammered iron gilded around the rim. The man was granite jawed and had tawny locks spilling from the back of his helmet and over his shoulders. As broad shouldered as a Minotaur and barrel chested, the towering man was wearing only a sleeveless shirt of chain mail, showing off his apish arms thick with muscle and rippling sinew, the veins resembling roots.

In his right hand, the warrior was carrying an over-sized spiked double-bladed ax that looked like it would take two men to wield. In his left was a large round shield. The helmet, ax, and shield were fashioned from the same dark metal and patterned with the same menacing designs.

The two-headed dog let out a throaty growl from one head and barked like thunder from the other. "Raawl-Ooolf!"

Zora slid so that she was hip to hip with Grey Cloak.

Drool dripped from the great dog's jaws. The brown beast looked part bulldog and part mastiff. One head had flat ears, and the other head's ears were pointed. A coat of thick hair covered his belly, and he had paws like a lion's. One of his front paws clawed at the dirt. Two stiff black tails wagged slowly behind its back. One head growled, and the other started sniffing.

The warrior set his eyes on Tatiana, and the beast crept toward her.

With her eyes widening, she said nervously, "Dalsay, I'm not going to stand here and be eaten."

Arm stretched out before him, Dalsay said in a stern voice, "Be still."

One of the dog's heads was the size of ten of Tatiana's.

The head with the lowered ears sniffed her face and hair, and slobber dripped onto her toes.

With her cheek turned aside, the elven mystic said, "Ew." The dog licked her face with a huge pink tongue. "Eeewwww." Then her tight expression softened. "But it feels so good."

In a strong voice oozing with confidence, the menacing warrior leaned forward in his saddle and said, "Chongo likes you, and I can see why. What manner of creature are you?"

Tatiana combed her hair behind her ear with a smile and said, "An elf."

With a glance at the amulet in her hand, the warrior asked, "Why did you summon me?" He twisted his ax in his grip. "I'm itching to kill something. Is it these men?" He gave Adanadel a hard-eyed stare. "Have they captured you?"

"No, it's not them." Tatiana pointed at the goblins. "It's them."

Chongo swung around one hundred eighty degrees. His rear end caused Tanlin and Adanadel to jump backward. The dog's head and ears lowered, and he started to growl at the goblins.

"More meat," the one-eyed goblin chieftain said. "Brothers, we shall feast like the kings of the Iron Hills tonight!"

The summoned warrior's nostrils flared, and the

muscles in his corded arms twitched. He set his eyes on the evil throng. "They look like underlings," he said as he raised his ax. "I hate underlings. Let's make some war! Eee-yah!"

Chongo leapt forward and sped toward the overwhelming goblin horde.

2

"Kill that dog!" the one-eyed goblin chieftain said.

Behind him, the other goblin chieftain barked orders to the goblins, and the mangy goblin war hounds sprinted toward Chongo. The goblin soldiers lowered their weapons and charged, and the dogs collided.

The warrior leapt from his saddle with his ax raised behind him. He sailed high and landed in the sea of blood-thirsty goblins. Moving with the ferocity of a metal panther, he spun around, creating a whirlwind of steel. The ax blades split through the goblins like butter.

It happened in a moment. Dyphestive stood flat footed and gaping as the warrior and his dogs slaughtered the goblins and the war dogs like sheep. He'd never seen a big man move so fast before. The ax cleaved heads from shoulders in a wink of an eye. Bones, armor, and skulls were hewn through like driftwood.

With his heart pumping like a racing horse, Dyphestive lifted his sword high. "What are we waiting for? Death to the goblins!" He charged.

"Time to kill some dirty acorns!" Browning said.

With Dyphestive leading the tip of the spear, Talon advanced on the goblins. Fire flew from Dalsay's fingertips, and streaks of deadly light blasted from Tatiana's hands.

Inspired by the warrior from another realm, Dyphestive blasted into a pack of goblins that broke from the fray. With a fierce swing of the iron sword, he cut through two of the wiry goblins. His sword went up and came down with force, and goblins jumped and dove out of the way.

"Triangle! Get into the triangle!" Adanadel ordered.

"Stay with me, boy!" Browning said as he absorbed a goblin hatchet swing on his shield. He punched a hole in his attacker's gut with his broad sword. "Tighten it up!"

The three men backed into a triangle formation.

Adanadel's smooth longsword strokes slipped into goblin bodies, and he smote them with the dagger in his other hand. Browning lunged and chopped. Fingers and necklace bones went flying. Dyphestive sawed back and forth, cutting a wide path deep through the ranks.

"There's so bloody many!" Browning called. "We'll be here all day killing them!"

"Work toward the chieftains! If we take them down, they might flee," Adanadel said.

"Or every goblin and chieftain will rain down on us!" Browning answered. He hacked a goblin down with a chop to the face. "Take that, you dirty acorn!"

Dyphestive's powerful arms kept swinging. The dead goblins began to stack up, but their numbers kept swelling. He eyeballed the chieftains barking orders. "Onward!"

A wave of goblins charged them in a wild-eyed attack. They burst through the triangle and separated the men.

Dalsay and Tatiana each held a large mystic shield in one hand and hurled streaks of energy with the other. The shields' golden energy shrugged off the goblin assault, but their mystic makeup began to crack.

Grey Cloak, Zora, and Tanlin were standing between the two magic users, attacking the advancing enemies. Zora hurled a blade into a goblin's throat then ducked another goblin's sword hack and stabbed him in the chest.

The quick-handed and sure-footed Tanlin was using a short sword and a dagger to battle the masses. "There are too many!"

"At least there are less than when we started," Grey Cloak said as he skipped away from a goblin lunging with a spear. He chopped into the goblin's backside and sent it dying on the ground. The goblins were strong and fast little men but not quicker than Grey Cloak. He saw their attacks before they came. The problem was so many attacking at once. He made a game out of it. *Dodge. Duck. Stab. Stab. Duck. Dodge.*

A club hurled through the air. Grey Cloak ducked. *Nice try.*

The club hit Zora in the back of the head, and she collapsed on the ground.

"Zora!" He jumped backward and swung his longsword into a spear-wielding goblin that was about to end her. "Die, goblin!"

"Everyone, stay together!" Dalsay ordered.

Grey Cloak helped Zora back to her feet. She was rubbing the back of her head. "You're supposed to duck."

"I don't have eyes in the back of my head," she fired back as she whipped a dagger from her belt and chucked it in between the eyes of a goblin. "Vermin!"

Dalsay and Tatiana locked hands, and a ring of silver light encircled the small group. A shimmering dome of magic energy covered the party.

From all directions, the enraged goblins hurled their bodies full force against the mystic dome and hit it with their crude weapons. A burly goblin head-butted the dome repeatedly with his small-horned helm. Others clawed at it and shrieked.

Dalsay's and Tatiana's fingers locked tight, the stress of

fighting the surging goblins visible on their distraught faces.

"Be strong, Tatiana. Be strong!" Dalsay said.

"I'm trying!" Tatiana's body shook as more goblins pounded the dome. Her knees wobbled. The dome began to crack. "I'm trying!"

3

"Argh!" Dyphestive cried as a hatchet sliced through the skin of his bare shoulders. He dropped his iron sword, snatched the goblin that had struck him, and put him in a headlock. Then he punched the goblin in the face, knocking its teeth out. "Take that!"

"Fight together!" Adanadel ordered. He swung his sword and his dagger in a deadly pattern that dropped goblin after goblin at his feet. "Gather!"

"There are too many!" Browning said. "We're all up to our necks and shoulders in goblins!" He split one's head open. "Gooey goblins, that is!"

Dyphestive balled up his big fists and started punching every wiry fiend that came at him. He walloped a goblin in the nose and elbowed another in the chest plate then picked up a third goblin and threw him at a charging trio.

Six goblins latched onto his legs, jumped onto his arms, and fought like demons to drag him to the ground.

"Get off of me!" Dyphestive said. He head-butted a goblin that dug its fingernails into his neck. The goblin fell away, clutching at his broken face. Dyphestive lifted two goblins from the ground, and they hung from his mighty arms. "How about a kiss?" He grabbed handfuls of their greasy hair and slammed their faces together.

"I can't fight them all off!" Browning yelled. His broadsword violently came down on a goblin charging him. "Whose idea was this, anyway?"

A spear sailed over the evil knot of fighters and hit Browning squarely in the chest, and his jaw dropped. The goblins' surge overwhelmed him.

"No!" Dyphestive screamed. "Nooo!" Goblins covered him from all directions. The sheer numbers overwhelmed him. His powerful legs gave out, and down to the ground he went.

"It doesn't look like you are ever going to have the pleasure of having that dinner with me," Grey Cloak said to Zora. They were standing back to back, eyeballing the swarm of goblins bent on crushing them. "It would have been a special occasion, with an abundance of mouthwatering pastries."

"How can you think about food at a time like this?" Zora asked. She was staring back at a goblin that had its eyes fixed on her. It was pointing its finger at her, gnashing its teeth and smacking its lips.

Grey Cloak shrugged. "I'm not the only one thinking about dinner."

Tanlin gave a hollow chuckle. "They say there is a time and place for everything. Perhaps laughing in the face of death is not a bad thing. I would have liked to have enjoyed a final meal before it all ended. And some elven wine. The best."

Grey Cloak nudged Zora. "See, I'm not crazy."

"Crazy isn't the word I had in mind," she replied. She slowly flipped her daggers. "Immature would be a better word for it."

"Me? Immature?"

Zora shook her head. "Dalsay! Tatiana! Is there anything that we can do?"

The wizard and the mystic were standing hand in hand with only the whites of their eyes showing. When the goblins jumped into the barrier, their bodies shook.

"No," Dalsay panted as if he was in great pain. "No."

Grey Cloak, Zora, and Tanlin made a ring around the magic users. They stood ready, with weapons brandished for the final attack. Grey Cloak's heart pounded in his ears. He didn't want to die. He'd never given it a thought, but suddenly, his life ending seemed inevitable. Swallowing his fear, he said, "Any last words?"

"Yes, be quiet," Zora said.

"Dog," Tanlin said.

"Dog?" Grey Cloak lifted an eyebrow. Outside of the dome, the huge two-headed dog, Chongo, plowed through the goblin ranks. "Dog! Go, dog! Go!"

Chongo's twin heads were filled with mouthfuls of goblins. He shook his thick neck, snapping the life out of the small men, and trampled over rows of goblins. His leonine paws ripped through the goblins' armor and tore flesh from their bones.

"Help, Chongo! Help!" Zora hollered.

As if the beast had understood her, Chongo skidded to a halt. Goblins swarmed him like ants, climbing his big body and jabbing their weapons into his pelt.

Chongo let out a loud "Raaaw-Uuulf!" He shook the goblins off like he was shedding water and set his hungry eyes on the ones attacking the dome.

The goblins gathered at the dome turned and looked at the charging beast. Suddenly, they started clawing at the dome in desperation, eyes wide with horror.

"They're scared!" Grey Cloak said. "Look at them. They want inside! Hah!"

Chongo swept around the edge of the dome, killing every goblin in his path. His powerful jaws ground them into goblin mud.

Grey Cloak, Zora, and Tanlin watched with fascination.

"I can't believe it," Tanlin said as he dropped to one knee. "The figurine worked. It worked!"

"So far, but what about the rest of us?" Zora asked.

Grey Cloak searched the battlefield for Dyphestive but saw only goblins and the warrior—no signs of anyone else. He pounded on the dome. "Let us out, Dalsay. Let us out!"

4

The goblins wrestled Dyphestive in a tangle of flesh. Claws and edged weapons tore at his body. He rolled over the violent brood, crushing them with his weight. But it didn't matter. They pinned his arms and legs and held him fast.

A goblin stood over him with his head cocked. He was holding a spear with the tip poised to strike. "You stole my chieftain's iron sword. Now, you will pay the price."

A spiked double-bladed ax ripped through the talking goblin's waist like butter. *Slice!*

The talking goblin's top half fell from the lower half, and the goblins pinning Dyphestive scattered.

Slice! Slice! Slice! Chop! Four goblins paid the ultimate price. They died from the ferocity of the summoned warrior's ax.

Dyphestive pushed up to a sitting position.

The helmeted warrior's blue eyes burned like fire when he looked at Dyphestive. In a robust voice, the warrior said, "You can fight better on your feet than on the ground." He set his eyes on the goblin chieftain and nodded. "Time to finish this."

When Dyphestive climbed to his feet, Adanadel was fighting his way to one knee, his head hanging. Dead goblins were sprawled out all around him.

Browning pulled a small spear out of his chest. With an agonized look on his pitted face, he said, "My blessed chain mail saved my tail end." He chucked the spear aside. "Again."

The warrior chopped a pathway through the last knot of goblins and squared off against the chieftains. One was bald and the other one eyed. The chieftains towered over the man. Each goblin carried a war hammer made from a solid piece of iron.

The goblins circled the warrior. For big goblins, they moved on lanky but nimble limbs. The bald goblin struck without warning, and the war hammer's head banged off of the warrior's shield. The powerful blow buckled the man's knees.

The one-eyed chieftain lashed out. His war hammer pounded the shield, one blow right after the other. The sound echoed loudly through the forest as they beat the warrior like a drum in perfect harmony. *Clang! Bang! Clang! Bang!*

"We have to help him," Dyphestive said to his weary colleagues. He searched for his sword and spotted the handle sticking out from underneath a pile of dead goblins. Keeping his eyes on the helmed warrior, he dashed toward the iron sword.

In a moment between war hammer strikes, the warrior spun underneath the chaos. He struck out like a cobra, his massive ax blades whistling through the air. *Slice! Slice!* The warrior chopped through the handles of both war hammers, leaving the chieftains swinging wildly at thin air. They stopped and gave dumfounded looks at the useless handles.

"The bigger they are, the sooner they'll fall." The warrior's ax blasted through the bald goblin's knees. The moaning goblin giant lowered to the ground chop by chop.

"Nooo! My brother!" The one-eyed goblin giant launched his ten-foot frame at the warrior.

The warrior impaled the huge giant on the spike of his ax and hoisted the brute high into the air. With muscle and veins popping in his chest and shoulders, he heaved the dead goblin chieftain aside.

Dyphestive marveled, looked at his comrades, and said, "I want to be him when I grow up."

The Iron Hills had become a field of the dead. Not a single goblin was left standing.

Dyphestive helped Browning to his feet. A wet spot of blood was on the man's chest. "Are you able?"

"I've been hurt worse," Browning said with a grunt. "I'll live." He surveyed their surroundings then looked at the gore-splattered warrior from another world. "Glad he was on our side."

The company gathered. Dyphestive could see that all of the members survived. The huge dog was licking the goblin grit off of Adanadel.

Dalsay and Tatiana spoke with the slayer from another world. They stood beside the figurine, which still remained upright on the ground.

"I summoned you, and I thank you, warrior. Can I have your name?" Tatiana asked.

Shaking the goblins' blood from his ax, the warrior said, "My enemies call me the Darkslayer, but you can call me Venir." He eyed Tatiana and smiled. "I've never kissed an elf before." He bent his head toward her. His body started to dissipate just as their lips almost touched. "Bish. Chongo has all of the fun."

Venir and Chongo's bodies quickly turned into smoke. Venir saluted with his ax. "Fight or die."

Chongo let out one final bark. "Raaawl-Uuulf!"

Then the wind carried the smoke away, and they were gone.

Tanlin let out a deep breath, dabbed the sweat from his

brow with a blue handkerchief, and said, "Phew, I thought we were dead."

Tatiana gave Dalsay an exhausted look. "You swore that you'd never bring the Figurine of Heroes again."

"Would you rather that I hadn't? We would have been dead without it," Dalsay said. He studied her dire expression then picked up the figurine and handed it to her. "Perhaps it would be best if you had to make the decision next time."

"There won't be a next time." Tatiana gave the figurine a hateful look and hurled it far into the woods. "Let the Iron Hills have it."

"Tatiana!" Dalsay said. "I understand your feelings, but that is a priceless artifact."

They started a heated argument, and the rest of the party backed away from the exchange.

Dyphestive said, "I don't want any part of this battle. It looks to be worse than the one we just faced. Does that figurine always summon such powerful creatures?"

"It's unpredictable," Adanadel answered. He cleaned his sword with a rag and sheathed it. "I'll tell you this. None of us has seen the likes of that slayer. Let alone his beast."

"Aye, I never thought the figurine would be enough in the first place," Browning said. He pulled off his coif, revealing a headful of sweat-soaked hair. "Look at all of those dead acorns. There're at least a hundred of them, and I only killed five myself."

"So what happened the last time that you used the figurine?" Grey Cloak asked. "Specifically?"

Tanlin frowned. "Tatiana's brothers were killed."

"Oh," Grey Cloak said. "Brothers?"

"Three of them. And that wasn't all."

"What killed them? Another warrior like that?" Dyphestive asked. The words came out before he noticed Tatiana's approach.

Tatiana glared at him and said, "We don't talk about the dead." She grabbed her pack and marched away. "*If* you want to find that cursed thing, you can do it without my help."

The company searched the woodland for over an hour, but the figurine didn't appear.

A frustrated Dalsay took one last look over the battlefield, shook his head, and said, "Perhaps she's right. Let's return to Raven Cliff."

5

RAVEN CLIFF

Talon had made it back to Raven Cliff only a day ago. Everyone was weary from the journey, and they'd agreed to meet up later in the day at the Red Claw Tavern. Dyphestive and Grey Cloak checked into an inn and had a full night's sleep. Finally, they had some money to their name, thanks to Grey Cloak's subtle hand. As for the trip back from the Iron Hills, it had been very quiet, except for Browning. He talked the entire time and was clearly the happiest to be alive after their harrowing journey.

Midmorning after their night of rest, the skies were clear, and the streets were a hive of activity. Merchants pushed their carts down the road, calling out sweet offers to all that passed them by. Burly laborers carried long lengths of timber on their shoulders. The smell of eggs, bacon, and mouthwatering biscuits intermingled with the perfumes that the pretty ladies sold on the streets.

"Excuse me. Excuse me," Grey Cloak said to an older man wearing a merchant's robes.

The human merchant had a double chin and a tiny moustache and wore fancy rings on all of his fingers. He sneered at Grey Cloak and said, "How can I help you? Can't you see that I am busy?"

"You have a store, right there, don't you?" Grey Cloak asked as he pointed at the door that the merchant was trying to unlock.

"Yes, and I'm late opening today." The man was breathing heavily, and perspiration built up on his forehead. "Long night entertaining my clients."

Grey Cloak pointed at the alley between the merchant's store and the next row of buildings. "There was a building there. Batram's Bartery and Arcania. Where is it?"

"Heavens, I don't know." The merchant turned the key in the door and pushed his body inside. "I have my own store to worry about. Why would I care about someone else's? Are you interested in purchasing some jewelry?"

"No."

"Then our conversation has concluded." The merchant shut the door in Grey Cloak's face.

Dyphestive was sitting on the end of the porch in the shade, chuckling.

"What are you laughing about?" Grey Cloak took a seat

beside his blood brother and scanned the streets. "I've asked at least ten people where Batram's is, and all of them gave me an ambiguous answer."

Scratching his chin, Dyphestive asked, "Are you sure this is the street?"

"This is Guild Row. I remember specifically. I remember the details. You know that." He tapped his foot on the cobblestone street. "How can an entire building disappear?"

Dyphestive shrugged.

"This really burns my cheeks. I have enough chips to buy my dagger back, but lo and behold, the entire building is gone." He brushed his hair behind his ear and looked over his shoulder. The alley where Batram's Bartery and Arcania should have been was vacant. "It makes no sense."

"Why don't you ask Dalsay? Or I could ask Tatiana for you," Dyphestive said with an excited smile.

"You would do anything to strike up a conversation with her, wouldn't you?"

"Yep."

"You can't fall in love with every beautiful woman that you see."

"I don't see why not."

"Of course you don't." Across the street, a group of laborers was unloading blocks of stone from horse-drawn wagons, and it made him think of Havenstock. For some reason, he missed it. "Besides, I don't really care to waste any more of my time in Dalsay's frosty company. He and Tatiana are together, you know. And they are fighting."

"I know. I'm not trying to steal his woman—I only like looking at her eyes and listening to her soft voice," Dyphestive said, and he turned his gaze to the small clouds passing through the sky. "She is so captivating. Don't you agree?"

Grey Cloak hopped up and started to pace behind his brother. "Any person with eyes would agree, but I have more important matters on my mind. Where is that bartery?"

"So what do you want to do?" Dyphestive asked. "Wait here all day for the store to magically appear? You have a good dagger and sword now."

"Not like that one. That dagger I stole from the gnoll was enchanted. And I didn't receive full value, only a smidgeon of its worth. Besides, its tip could pierce stone, and it was so light in my hand." Grey Cloak squatted down beside his brother. "Not to mention all of the other marvelous items that he carried. Perhaps I can buy something else that will benefit me... I mean us."

Across the street, a team of horses pulled the empty wagons out and rode down the street. Their hooves clopped loudly on the cobblestones.

"I miss shoeing horses," Dyphestive said.

"Do you have any ambition at all?"

"Of course I do. That doesn't mean I can't miss doing something."

Grey Cloak hopped off the porch and onto the street. He stood with his back to Dyphestive. "I'm tired of being shortchanged. Dalsay only gave us a meager portion of what was owed to us from the temple. Not to mention that Zora robbed me not once but twice. I won't let that happen again."

Dyphestive interlocked his fingers, pushed out, and cracked his knuckles. The pop was so loud that a woman walking by jumped away from him. He looked back at the woman and said, "Sorry."

Grey Cloak turned around. "I told you not to do that. It startles... peop..." He gazed at the alley. A sign was hanging from a strange building that filled the void that was once there. The sign read Batram's Bartery and Arcania. He stared at the black door, which seemed to stare back at him, then he shook Dyphestive's shoulder and pointed at the door.

"Whoa!" Dyphestive said.

The black door swung open. Someone with a cheery voice called from within, "Open for business."

6

IRON HILLS

Drysis the Dreadful surveyed the carnage on the ground. Scores of goblins and two formidable chieftains had been slaughtered. The white-haired warrior woman, armored in dyed-black leather armor, fanned away the buzzing flies with her arm that was covered in chain mail. "Death. Goblins. Disgusting." She dismounted her gourn, a horse-like creature that was built like a horse but had a dragon head and scales, and carefully navigated the field of the dead.

Joining her were four other warriors, Doom Riders. All of the imposing men wore dyed leather skull masks and were armored in leather that looked like dragon scales. Each of them carried their personal assortment of weapons. Like her, they dismounted their gourns and waded through the buzzing insects.

Groups of vultures that had been dining on the dead beat their wings and scattered, squawking, and flew into the branches of the nearby trees.

One of the Doom Riders, who wore a red skull mask, picked up a goblin arm and held it out. In a raspy voice, he said, "This cut is as clean as any cut I've ever seen. Only a special weapon would do this. The striplings we seek, they travel with men that are very formidable."

"You sound scared, Blood Scar."

Blood Scar gave a dry laugh. "Huh. I like a challenge."

The Doom Rider with a grass-green mask stood over the one-eyed goblin chieftain. He grabbed the goblin by the hair and lifted the body. "Goblin chiefs aren't slouches. This one has a hole in his heart. Heh-heh. And he was tossed like a log from that spot"—he pointed a few yards away—"to this one. That's extraordinary."

"I'm not blind, Shamrok," Drysis said.

"I wasn't suggesting you were, fearless leader, but you have to admire the handiwork that was wrought here." Shamrok grunted. "I only want to be prepared for what we are facing."

The Doom Rider in the blue skull mask didn't say anything at all. Instead, he picked his way through the bodies, paying no mind to the insects buzzing in his face. He stood with his hands balled up under his chin, looking down at two goblins that had been torn apart by something more savage than weapons. In a bookish manner, he spoke.

"A beast bigger than the goblin war hounds did this. Whatever it was, it disappeared."

Drysis raised an eyebrow. "Interesting, Ghost." She flipped up the eye patch that covered her right eye and studied the ground using the magic of her eye. She'd sacrificed her eye for an enchanted power that allowed her to see more than what the natural eye revealed. After following the boot prints on the ground, she gazed at where Ghost was standing. "Interesting."

Lion-like paw prints bigger than that of the war hounds were on the ground.

"Perhaps it was a chimera," she suggested.

"There weren't any chimera prints leading up to this spot, and I don't see any prints leaving, either," Shamrok said. "The company we chase, I think they were aided somehow."

"It's clear that they have a wizard among them," she said. "We figured that out at the temple at Crow Valley." Her jaw clenched. "It seems that we just missed crossing paths with our prey. So close, but we will have them. It appears that they are heading back to where they started in Raven Cliff. Saddle up. It's time to ride." She flipped her eye patch down. "Our chase is coming to an end."

"Raven Cliff, huh. Excellent, I could use some good eating," Shamrok said as he climbed into the saddle of his dragon horse. "I'm buying."

Drysis climbed onto her horse. "Don't get so excited.

We aren't going to ride into town and start kicking doors down."

"Why not?" Blood Scar asked. "Don't you like seeing the terror on people's faces?"

"Of course, but these two striplings have slipped us for three years. Now that we are so close, it's time to cast a wide net so that they don't see us coming." She patted her gourn's neck, and it moved forward. "Black Frost has allies in all places. We'll use them to our advantage."

The Doom Riders rode day and night, not stopping until they made it to the outskirts of Raven Cliff. Less than a league away, they made camp where they could see the bustling city resting on the cliffs.

In the dead of night, Ghost tossed a small pouch into the campfire flames. The fire made a bright-blue flash, and an imp no taller than his finger rose out of the flames. The imp was an ugly thing with rough spots all over his body. His mosquito wings beat, and he flew over to Drysis.

"Notify the servants of Black Frost. Tell them to bring supplies. We wait."

The imp nodded. His blue body winked like the light of a firefly, and he buzzed toward the city, a tiny blue streak in the night.

7

———

RAVEN CLIFF

"Welcome!" the razorback hog rug that lay at the entrance to the arcania said.

Grey Cloak and Dyphestive hopped over it and stood at the front counter of the store. Behind the black wood counter were rows of shelving and drawers that were stacked up to the top of a thirty-foot-high ceiling. The wooden drawers were the same black mahogany as the front counter. Each of them had a corroded brass handle. The drawers at the bottom were as big as coffins, and they became smaller the farther that they were.

"Hello?" Grey Cloak called as he set his eyes on the webbing on the top set of drawers. That was the place that the creepy little store owner, Batram, had slunk down from the last time they met. "Hello? Batram?"

"I'm coming!" Batram said in an irritated voice.

Behind the counter and down the hallway, a halfling man was walking toward them, carrying a brass candleholder and wearing a sleeping gown and a cap with little spiders woven into it. From the other side of the counter, Batram climbed up a stepladder and sat down on the counter. The white-haired halfling yawned and rubbed his eyes.

"I'm not used to being up so early," Batram said. He blew out the candle and set the holder down then pushed aside the fuzzy black ball from his nightcap that had been hanging between his eyes. He blinked and looked at Grey Cloak. "What do you want?"

"I came to pay the fee on my dagger," Grey Cloak said as he gave his brother a concerned look.

"A dagger? I have many daggers," Batram said. "You need to be more specific."

Grey Cloak looked the halfling in the eye. "Don't you remember us? We were just here over a week ago. I'm Grey Cloak, and this is Dyphestive."

"Hello," Dyphestive said.

Batram's bushy white eyebrows wiggled when he blinked. "Oh yes, the elf named after the garment. Classy. All I need is your receipt of sale."

"Receipt of sale?" Grey Cloak asked.

"Why yes, every time you exchange a rare commodity, you are going to want a record of it. It's called bookkeeping. I have my spiders do it." He pointed at the end of the long counter. A tarantula as big as Dyphestive's hand was holding a quill and scribbling down something on parchment.

Grey Cloak and Dyphestive both did a double take.

"What is your fascination with spiders?" Grey Cloak asked.

"Nothing," Batram said. He had changed to have six arms and six sleeves. "But they are very useful pets. Now, the receipt."

"I don't have a receipt. You didn't give me one," Grey Cloak said as his jaw tightened.

"Hmmm..." The halfling rubbed his chin and started speaking under his breath. "I always give a receipt, unless the circumstances are extenuating. Let's see, I was in a hurry, I was sleepy, hungry, or—" He snapped the fingers on his other five hands. "I remember. I was positively certain that you were not going to return. Yeah, that's the ticket."

Grey Cloak rose on tiptoe so his chin was even higher above the large counter. "I'm here now, and I want my dagger."

"Don't get testy with me, stripling. This is my store. My rules."

"How do you make your store disappear?" Dyphestive asked.

"That's not any of your business, but it's a brilliant way to keep robbers out, now isn't it?"

Dyphestive shrugged. "I suppose."

"Yes, you can't steal what you can't see. Now, let me see, where did I put that dagger? I have many daggers." Batram stood and walked down the countertop, eyeing the drawers. "I hope that I didn't sell it when I made the assumption that you would not be back."

"You didn't sell it, did you?" Grey Cloak's cheeks reddened.

"What did you expect? I'm a businessman, and by the looks of you, you weren't coming back. No shoes, holes in your clothing. I get your kinds all the time. Urchins that pilfer in the streets and quickly cash in. I never thought the likes of you would make it back, unless you wanted to sell something. You don't have anything else to sell, do you?"

"Do you have my dagger or not?"

"Do you have the twenty-five silver chips that I lent you?"

Grey Cloak slapped down a pile of silver coins on the countertop.

Batram hurried back across the counter and looked at the coins. "My, where did you get all of that? Did you steal it?"

"No," Grey Cloak fired back.

Batram looked at Dyphestive. "Did he steal it?"

"Can you steal from the dead?"

"Dyphestive, keep your mouth shut." Grey Cloak fought to regain his composure and sucked through his teeth.

"Batram, we are adventurers. This is part of what we earned from our last quest."

"I see." Batram leaned over the counter and looked them up and down. "You wear and carry like men, and you have an air about you too." He rubbed his chin with two left hands and tapped his bare toes on the counter. "Hmph, I believe you. Sad, very sad."

Grey Cloak and Dyphestive exchanged a curious look.

"What's so *sad*?" Grey Cloak asked.

"Your dagger. I sold it."

8

____

Grey Cloak slapped his hands on the counter and yelled, "*What?*"

"Mind your temper, little elf, or I'll have you removed from my store—permanently," Batram warned. "Besides, it was an honest mistake. If you were in my position, you would have done the same thing. I'll tell you what... I'll give you another twenty-five chips, and we'll call it even." He extended his small long-fingered hand. "Deal?"

"Do you take me for some kind of fool? I want my dagger back. It's not my fault that you sold it, you cotton-headed quarry gnome," Grey Cloak said.

"There is no need to be insulting." Batram grew into a ten-foot-tall spiderlike creature with eight ruby-red eyes and long, hairy insect arms. "I've warned you about taking that tone with me."

Dyphestive stepped backward with his mouth gaping.

Grey Cloak stood his ground and poked his finger on the counter. "I'm not leaving until I receive what is owed to me. You owe me one enchanted dagger. I'll have it now."

"That's not a very good counteroffer," Batram said. His spidery fingers on his second set of lower legs drummed on the counter. "You need to improve your negotiation skills. And control your temper."

"A counteroffer? All right, one hundred gold pieces."

"No, that's not a very good price. Hmm..." Batram reached over the counter, grabbed the hood of Grey Cloak's cloak, and pulled it off.

"What are you doing?" Grey Cloak asked. "Give me that back."

Batram flipped the cloak like a rug. "This is a pitiful garment. Perhaps I can offer you something far better. It won't have moth holes in it." He turned around, and his spidery arms started opening and closing the drawers. "No. No. No. No." He tossed the cloak aside. It floated through the air and hooked on a peg between the shelving.

Dyphestive squatted and looked inside the counter's glass casing. "Look at this."

"What?" Grey Cloak squatted, too, and looked inside the case. A group of five throwing knives lay in a fanned-out pattern. A dagger with a golden hilt had a whale's head on the pommel. A pair of short swords with black blades with a layering pattern in the metal were next to ivory and jade figurines of wild animals and soldiers from many races. A huge tooth accompanied by smaller ones made a necklace. Grey Cloak stood up. "I'll take the pair of short swords."

"Huh?" Batram was back in halfling form again, with only two arms. "Those aren't for sale, but I think you'll like this." A gray cloak was draped over his small extended arms. "A gray cloak, like the one that you wear but much better."

"I have a cloak, and I don't need another one." He eyed the garment. It was well knitted and didn't show any seams. He touched the cloak and rubbed it between his fingers. The cloth had a silky feel, like a soft animal pelt. "What does it do?"

"Ah, this cloak does many things. Many, many things." He gave a wicked chuckle. "It keeps you warm on cold nights and shields you from the wind and rain."

Dyphestive stood up, tilted his head to one side, and said, "Don't all cloaks do that?"

"Of course they do." Grey Cloak gave his brother an irritated glance. "He's trying to buffalo me again."

"No, no, no, stripling, I make fair exchanges." Batram pushed the cloak at the elf. "Try it on. You'll see for yourself. This cloak was made by elven monks from Green Hills of Arrowwood." His voice lowered, and he made an impish expression. "Very special. Very unique."

Grey Cloak took the hooded cape, let the folds drop to

the floor, and in a smooth motion, swung it over his shoulders. He tied the two black cords of leather at the neck and shifted inside the gray garment.

"It's nice—not too nice, like a rich man from Portham, but good," Dyphestive commented. "How does it feel?"

Grey Cloak leaned his head back and forth, and with a frown, he said, "It's comfortable. Warm. But a good cloak is supposed be comfortable and warm. That's hardly anything extraordinary. It's high quality, nothing more, nothing less."

With his light eyes shining, Batram said, "But you like it, yes?"

"I like it, but I don't think it's worth the price of an enchanted dagger. Does it do anything else at all?" He noticed two pockets in the front, and he searched the inside lining. The lining was the same material on the inside as the outside. "I had small pockets in my other cloak."

"Take it to a seamstress."

"So it's an ordinary cloak."

"Made by elven sages."

"You said monks," Dyphestive said.

"One or the other, I don't know for certain which." Batram frowned. "Do you want it or not?"

"Will it turn me invisible?" Grey Cloak quipped.

Batram reached behind Grey Cloak, grabbed the hood, and covered his head. "There, your head is no longer visible. Do we have a deal?"

Dyphestive rumbled with laughter.

"Ha-ha." Grey Cloak lifted the hood from his face and started untying the cords of the cloak. "I'll take back mine."

"No, wait. I'll make a deal with you. You keep the cloak as collateral, and I'll see what I can do to get your dagger back."

"Sure. You and my dagger will disappear again." Grey Cloak did like the cloak, but he wasn't going to admit it. "I'll give you a week. And when I come back, you have my dagger, or I keep this cloak and one hundred gold pieces."

"Make it two weeks and fifty gold pieces and the cloak." Batram stuck his hand out.

Grey Cloak shook his small hand, smiled, and said, "I'm going to need that in writing."

9

___

Rhonna the dwarven blacksmith was standing outside of the front door of an abandoned wooden shack. The small building was half covered in ivy, and wild flowers grew around the edges. It was late in the day, and the sun had dipped behind the trees, casting shade on the grove where the shack stood.

"Are you certain this is where he lived?" Rhonna asked.

Lythlenion the orcen cleric replied, "This is the last place where I met with him." He was standing behind her, his big frame hanging over her shoulder, wearing a metal breastplate and carrying a two-handed studded mace. "Did you knock?"

"Yes," she said. "Didn't you hear me?"

"I must have been distracted by the birds. I love the

songs that they sing in the wild. It's not like that near the oceans. The seabirds don't carry a tune."

She pushed the battered door open with her stubby fingers, and it groaned on its hinges. The windowless shack was dim inside. With a dagger in hand, she moved into the opening. The door raked over the overgrowth underneath it. The room was barely big enough for them to stand in.

"I told you it was small. Bowbreaker is not fond of indoor places, unless the rain is heavy or a great deal of snow is falling," Lythlenion said. He blinked his big eyes. "I told you that it's been a while since I've seen him."

"Yes, I know," she said. She looked around for any clue of life at all. There were no shelves, pots, or pans, or a cup of any sort, for the matter. "Strange, though. I don't see where anything else has made a home of this spot. You would think that the varmints would have taken it over." She pointed to a corner. "I don't even see silk spiders."

Lythlenion nodded. "Hmph, that's true. Well, maybe Bowbreaker is near. We only need to wait for him to appear. It's getting late. Should I make a fire?"

Rhonna moved back outside and eyed the woodland. There was never any telling when Bowbreaker would show up. He could have been leagues away, for all she knew. "We'll give him one night. Besides, I need you to work your craft. That's more important."

Lythlenion rubbed his hands together. "It's been a while. I'll do my best." He started a fire, boiled rice in a small pot, and sprinkled in some wild onions he'd pulled from the ground.

Rhonna snapped the necks of a pair of rabbits and skinned them then put them on spits over the campfire flames. She sat back and listened to Lythlenion talk.

"Lylith is a pretty little thing, isn't she? I always hoped I would have a daughter, but I needed a wife first. I have to admit that I'm surprised that Sarah took to me." Lythlenion grinned. "I'm not what you would call a handsome fella. Of course, orcs aren't known for their charm and good looks, not like dwarves." He waved his hand in front of Rhonna. "Are you listening?"

Rhonna caught herself staring into the fire. "Huh? Yes... no." She shook her head. "My mind is set on those boys." She turned one of the rabbits. "I can't believe Doom Riders are after them. Doom Riders. To make matters worse, Drysis is one of them."

"This really bothers you, doesn't it?"

"The fact that I might have to scrape against a former ally. She was always an icy woman, but I never saw this coming. She serves Black Frost. No one good serves that dragon."

"You think those boys are special?"

"They wouldn't come after them if they weren't. I should have known better when I took them in. They came out of nowhere. Something was off about them. Especially Grey Cloak. He was always cocky and secretive."

"Sounds like a typical stripling." He shook his head. "Ah, I hope my precious Lylith never grows up."

They ate all of the rabbit meat and emptied the pot of rice and vegetables. The coals on the fire grew dim.

"Can you do your magic?" Rhonna asked as she wiggled her fingers over the fire.

"Yes, but I need some personal belongings from the youths. At least one of them. Didn't you say that the Doom Riders took a blanket?"

"I did." She reached behind her and grabbed her pack. "The boys didn't have much, but Dyphestive had a pair of shoes that he came with as a boy." She pulled out a leather loafer that had a hole in the big toe. "He wore them until his feet almost busted out of them. Well, his foot did bust one of them, and I threw it away. I'm not really sure why this one survived, but it did." She tossed it to Lythlenion.

Lythlenion snatched the shoe out of the air. "Perhaps that boy kept it as a keepsake, or you did?"

"I'm not worried about an old shoe."

"Sure," he said politely. "In order to cast the spell, I'll have to destroy the shoe."

"I'll live."

He chuckled. From his pack, he removed a soft leather pouch. For an orc, he had soft features, and hands to go with them. He gently reached into the pouch and grabbed a large pinch of a tobacco-like substance that had purple bits that glittered in it. He sprinkled it over the campfire flames, closed his eyes, and started chanting arcane words that rolled off his tongue.

The campfire flames spit and hissed, and the orange turned deep purple. Smoke twisted above the flames in a spiral toward the sky.

Lythlenion dropped the shoe in the fire, and the hungry flames engulfed the worn leather. The fire lifted the shoe, suspending it on a bed of flame.

Rhonna's eyes widened. She didn't care for magic. If it wasn't controlled, it could cause more harm than good. She scooted back from the fire.

The purple flames began eating away the leather like the hungry mouth of a living thing. The shoe turned to ashes, and the ashes merged with the smoke and drifted higher into the air.

Lythlenion watched the smoke trail making its way through the branches and into the sky. Then the purple fire flickered and flashed and turned back to its natural glow.

"Now what?" Rhonna said. "Seems to me nothing happened."

"We wait," he said with a warm smile on his face. His shoulders sagged as he exhaled deeply. "It's been a long time since I've fooled with my craft." He stretched out his arms and yawned. "Tiring."

"Do you need a nap?" she asked in a mocking voice.

"It wouldn't hurt."

A soft rustle deeper in the woodland caught Rhonna's ear. She stood up and drew her knife.

Lythlenion gave her a curious look and whispered, "What is it?"

"We have company."

10

The evening breeze was replaced by eerie stillness.

Lythlenion slid his war hammer across the grass and brought it up to his chest as he rose.

In the forest line beyond the flames, a branch snapped, and something pushed through the trees. Something big.

Rhonna sheathed her dagger and picked up her hammer, which had been lying on the ground nearby. She had crafted the weapon herself. It had a flat head of steel on one end and a cone-shaped spike on the other. Its handle was made of solid black oak and fit her two-handed grip. Grooves from her hand were worn in the wood. As the creature pushed its way through the forest, her hammer suddenly felt small in her viselike grip.

"Perhaps we should hide," Lythlenion said as he backed away from the sound and stood behind her.

"Have you ever known me to hide from anything?" she replied under her breath. She backed up farther. "Besides, whatever it is knows we are here."

Lythlenion rolled the handle of his war mace in his hand. It had a flanged metal head and a two-handed handle and was made of sturdy material the same as his breastplate. "It sounds big. Perhaps it only seems that way because it's night."

"I don't think so. I think it sounds big because it is big." Her nostrils flared. "Mm-hmm, it's big," she said in a gravelly voice. "The question is how big."

Branches in the black shadows of the woodland started to crack and pop as the creature closed in on them.

Rhonna's heart thumped rapidly. She was on a search-and-rescue mission, not a search-and-destroy quest. She'd hoped to avoid any dangerous encounters. Tightening her grip on her war hammer, she thought of every possible scenario. Barely above a whisper, she said, "When it comes, follow my lead."

He nodded.

The interlocked branches of the maple trees rustled and pushed forward. Twelve feet high in the leaves, the face of a giant emerged. He pushed through the branches, revealing the entirety of his scary face. His long, shaggy hair hung down over his eyes, and his nose was large and protruding. The bare-chested brute wore only animal skins over his waist. He moved his head from side to side and sniffed so loudly the campfire flames flickered.

"Holy horseshoes," Rhonna muttered.

The wild giant grunted, "Uhmmm..."

Rhonna gritted her teeth. The towering menace was a called a skuurd, a breed of wild giants that roamed the land. She hadn't seen one since she was a child. They were fierce flesh-eating brutes with ravenous appetites and no mercy in them.

The skuurd pushed his hair away from his eyes, revealing two oversized orbs that were pitch black. He cast his hungry gaze on Rhonna and Lythlenion. His smile showed off his rows of rotting yellow teeth. Rubbing his stomach, he smacked his lips. "Mmm... I'm going to eat well tonight."

"Yes, we have all of the rice that you can handle," Lythlenion offered.

The wild giant pulled his shoulders back and stood upright. "You offer me, Gartun, rice? I will eat you headfirst, orc."

"This isn't what I had in mind when I set out on this adventure," Lythlenion whispered to Rhonna. "What is a skuurd doing in these parts?"

"You're asking me?"

"Let's make this easy," the deep-voiced giant said. He reached back and tore a branch off a tree like it was a sapling. "I'll make a spit, you stand still, and I'll put you on it. That way I can cook you over the fire that you prepared for me."

"You're going to need a bigger fire than that one," Lythlenion said with a shaky voice. "We would be happy to fetch you more firewood."

"Stay put!" Gartun said. "I am fast. I'll track you down and stomp you into the ground. I will break every bone in your fragile bodies."

Under her breath, Rhonna said to Lythlenion, "Go for the nanoos."

"What?"

She eyed the giant's lower extremities and tipped her head. "The nanoos."

"Ah, the beans. I understand." He gave her a curious look. "Now?"

"No, follow my lead." She moved toward the giant and lifted her arms and hammer over her head. "Oh, mighty Gartun, let me be the first to surrender. For I know that we are no match for you. Take me first, over this orc. Everyone knows that dwarfs taste better than orcs."

"A wise dwarf. One that does not put up a fight or a chase. Perhaps tonight is my night," the skuurd huffed. "Stand still, small one. You can be my appetizer." Gartun reached down with his massive hands. His gnarled fingers were thick like tree roots.

Rhonna eyeballed the giant's big toe. As the wild giant's hands fell around her body, she shouted at the top of her lungs, "Now!" She brought her hammer down with all of her might. The spiked head of the hammer hit the giant's toe on the sweet spot between the nail and the skin.

Gartun threw his hands up and let out a howl. He hopped on one foot and tried to hold the bad foot.

Lythlenion raced past the campfire. He struck the giant full force in the crotch with his war hammer, and the giant doubled over and let out an agonized groan. With a hard swing of her hammer, Rhonna connected with the giant's temple. His knees wobbled, and he fell to the ground.

"A good plan!" Lythlenion cocked back his war hammer to deliver a lethal blow. "We'll break this giant's bones tonight!"

From his hands and knees, Gartun gave a wide, desperate swipe. He knocked Rhonna and Lythlenion clear off of their feet, and they fell hard to the ground, but they immediately scrambled up to their feet.

They weren't the only ones to rise. Gartun got back to his feet as quickly as they did. He glowered down at both of them, gnashed his teeth, and said, "You're both dead!"

11

Gartun lunged at Lythlenion, who jumped away, only to have the wild giant snag him by the ankle. The giant dragged him across the ground with one arm, like a man handling a child half his size.

Rhonna charged the giant and swung her hammer into the knuckle of his free hand, but

Gartun jerked his hand away, gave her the evil eye, and backhanded her. She tumbled head over heels and skidded into a tree so hard that acorns fell. Shaking the hazy stars from her eyes, she climbed back to her feet.

Gartun the giant picked Lythlenion up with both hands and shook him like a rag. "You hurt me... now I will hurt you!"

An arrow with black feathers whistled through the air

and struck Gartun in the right eye. A second arrow zipped into the giant's left eye.

Gartun dropped Lythlenion and roared like a wounded lion. *"Raaawrrr!"* He clutched at the arrows sticking out of his face and ripped them both out. "I'm blinded! I'm blinded!"

Two more arrows buried themselves feather deep in the meat of the giant's hairy chest.

Thunk! Thunk!

The skuurd's legs wobbled, and he stumbled through the grove, screaming and clutching at the branches. His big body fell through the limbs and snapped them away, and he lay with his back against a tree, his chest heaving.

"I won't die," Gartun said. "I can't die. I'm skuurd. We live phff..." His body convulsed, then he let out his final breath and died.

Rhonna hustled over to the shaken Lythlenion and helped him to his feet. "How are you?"

"Dizzy but not dead. I'll take it," he said.

She handed him his war hammer and turned to see the giant's killer. A male elf walked out of the woodland. He was wearing buckskin clothing, had long brown hair and green eyes, and was carrying a longbow made of black ash wood, and a quiver full of arrows with black feathers hung from his back. The only other things he was wearing were a long hunting knife that hung from his waist to his knee and high hunting boots made from bear leather.

"Rhonna. Lythlenion," the stone-faced elf said. He had strong angular features. His buckskin only covered his left arm, and his right one was noticeably bigger than the left. "You owe me four moon-head arrows."

"Nice to see you, too, Bowbreaker," Rhonna said.

Bowbreaker made his way over to the skuurd giant. He put his hand behind the giant's neck. "He's dead. Sometimes they play dead." He broke off his arrows and tossed them in the fire. "I don't want to get blamed for this one too."

"Hello, Bowbreaker," Lythlenion said as he offered his hand. "You couldn't have come at a better time. I'm thankful for your timely arrival."

"Next time you fight a skuurd, you might want to try another plan. Hitting them in the beans isn't the best one," Bowbreaker said. He sat down cross-legged in front of the fire.

"Hold on a moment," Rhonna said. "You were watching?"

"Of course I was. You were the bait."

"*Bait?* I ought to bust you in the mouth, you reckless ranger."

"No one was hurt. Lythlenion, are you hurt?"

The orc shook his head.

"And you, Rhonna?" Bowbreaker asked politely.

"No, but *you* are going to be."

"I don't think so. Now, tell me, what brings you to my

wood? I hope it's a friendly visit, but let me guess... you have another quest. I told you before—I'm finished with that sort of thing. I don't care for material pleasure. I have all I need in the wood."

"We are searching for a pair of striplings. A human and an elf. Black Frost wants them," she said.

Bowbreaker nodded. "And you want me to help you track them down? Did Lythlenion cast a spell to do that?"

"You saw that?" Lythlenion asked, surprised.

"He's probably been following us since we broke his wood line," Rhonna said. "Still as sly as a serpent."

"It's what I do." A squirrel scurried across the ground with a small branch filled with large blueberries. Bowbreaker patted the squirrel on the head and gave him a berry. The squirrel stuffed the large berry in his mouth and darted into the darkness. Bowbreaker started eating the berries. "Go ahead and tell me more about these boys."

"Black Frost sent Doom Riders after them. The lead Doom Rider is one that we know. Drysis," Rhonna said.

The normally stoic elf raised his eyebrows. "Drysis is a Doom Rider. I can't believe it."

"She killed a friend of mine in cold blood. She's all business—made that perfectly clear to me."

"Sounds like she wanted you to stay out of it," Bowbreaker said, "but here you are. But why come to me if you can track them?"

"I'm more blacksmith than fighter, and your tracking is

an advantage, but if we cross Drysis, we could use more muscle. And... well, you know," she said.

"Drysis and I were a long time ago. I chose the wood over her. Perhaps that was a mistake." Bowbreaker ate another berry. "But I don't have any desire to cross her or the Doom Riders. I've seen what the likes of them can do. Not to mention the gourn. This is a situation that I would rather stay out of."

Rhonna sat down and said, "Well, that's great."

The campfire's flames turned purple and brightened, and an image formed inside them.

Lythlenion dropped to his knees by the fire. "My spell is complete. Watch."

In the flickering flames, a city resting on cliffs appeared.

"Raven Cliff," Rhonna said. "Wouldn't you agree?"

"I do," Lythlenion said. He slapped her shoulder with the back of his hand. "And it's not so far away."

Dyphestive appeared in the crowded streets. Grey Cloak was with him, and their faces had painful grimaces. The images faded away.

"What happened?" she asked. "Are they in danger?"

"I don't know. It could be the present or the past we see," Lythlenion said. "At least Raven Cliff isn't so far away."

"We're leaving now, with or without you, Bowbreaker." She looked back at the spot where Bowbreaker had been sitting, but the elven ranger was gone.

12

Grey Cloak was sitting at a table inside the Red Claw Tavern, accompanied by Dyphestive and Browning. Dyphestive was sawing into a steak that filled his metal plate, and Browning was drinking a flagon of ale.

The Red Claw Tavern was a dimly lit tavern made out of a cave within the cliff face of Raven Cliff. A traveler didn't take a typical beaten path to get there. Patrons had to walk down the wooden decking and stairs. However, the Red Claw Tavern wasn't for the commoner, but rather, for hardened travelers and adventurers that preferred discretion. Men and women were huddled over their tables, talking quietly in some cases, while others talked loudly, jested, and sang dreadfully.

Grey Cloak fingered the small pockets inside his cloak. He hadn't noticed them when he initially acquired it from

Batram. He slipped a coin in one pocket slit and pulled it out of another pocket. *Interesting. I like it. Did Batram know about this?*

Wiping the froth off of his mouth, Browning said, "You're very quiet, elf."

He closed his cloak over his chest. "Well, I thought you could use a break from all of my chattering."

Browning shrugged. "I don't know which is worse. Your talking or this one's eating." He looked at Dyphestive, who was devouring huge chunks of steak and potatoes in one bite. He gave the young man a hearty slap on the back. "Next time order the entire cow, why don't you." He grimaced.

Dyphestive swallowed his food and said, "Is that wound still bothering you, Browning?"

"I'll be fine. I'm getting old and don't bounce back like I used to." He flagged down a barmaid. "I'll take another, sweetie."

"Is this what we do? Sit here and wait and see when we hear from Dalsay?" Grey Cloak asked as he eyed his surroundings.

Two drunken men were bumping chests as they fought over an orcen woman. Butterlip the ogre bouncer silently crept out of his nook beside the front door. The towering ogre grabbed each man by the back of his head, and he bumped their heads together.

"Ouch," Grey Cloak said.

Browning chuckled.

Butterlip's huge hands pinched the men on the napes of their necks. He shoved them toward the red front door and escorted them outside. When he came back in the door, he glared at the watching crowd and said in a grisly voice, "Behave yourself!" Then he sank back into his alcove.

"Maybe we should take him on one of our adventures," Grey Cloak quipped.

"You don't want that. He would eat all of the food and take all of the treasure. But in a scrape like that last one we were in, you would definitely want him on yer side," Browning answered.

The barmaid arrived with another flagon with white froth oozing over the rim.

"There you are, dear. That looks delicious." He leaned back and hitched his arm over the back of the chair. "As I was saying, ogres are great fighters but not the best company. I've traveled with them before. They aren't very good at taking orders."

"I'm sure Dalsay would hate that," Grey Cloak said. "He isn't very amiable."

"He is what he is. You get used to it," Browning said then gulped down part of his ale. "Ah, that's good."

"So what are we supposed to do? Wait around for Dalsay between adventures? I thought that we were supposed to be catching a dragon."

"I figure we are working our way up to that."

Teetering on the back two chair legs, Browning shrugged. "It is what it is. In the meantime, we meet here once every couple of weeks, like we are now, and we live our ordinary lives." He tapped his chest with a fist and belched. "I'm usually here, though. I score enough chips to tide me over between adventures. Besides, I like it here."

"What does Tatiana do?" Dyphestive blurted.

"Someone is really sweet on the elf, isn't he? Well, that's Dalsay's lady now. You might want to pick a woman closer to your years, young fella. Like Zora."

Dyphestive and Grey Cloak exchanged glances.

"I don't think my brother would like that."

"Why would I care?" Grey Cloak asked.

"Because you are as sweet as a bear on honey when it comes to Zora," Dyphestive said.

"Is someone talking about me?" Zora asked. She had come out of nowhere, and she turned a chair around and sat down at the table between Grey Cloak and Dyphestive.

"Where did you come from?" Grey Cloak asked. It drove him crazy that she always managed to slip up on him without him noticing.

She rubbed his head and said, "Ah, did someone overlook me? Tee-hee. I've been here since before you arrived. I work here as well as Tanlin's shop. I like to stay in the back and cook. How's your steak, Dyphestive?"

"Perfect."

"You're welcome," she replied. "So what are we talking about?"

"Nothing," Grey Cloak said.

"They were talking about how much Grey Cloak likes you and how much Dyphestive likes Tatiana."

"She's old enough to be your mother, Dyphestive," she said playfully.

Dyphestive blushed. "I don't want to marry her. I only think she is very pretty."

"Sure. But you might want to mind yourself. Dalsay is very protective of her."

"What happened to her brothers?" Grey Cloak asked. He hadn't forgotten the argument between Tatiana and Dalsay over the Figurine of Heroes. "I suppose Dalsay is to blame for that."

"Well, I wasn't there." She grabbed one of the chunks of Dyphestive's seasoned potatoes with her fingers. "But Browning was."

"I ain't telling," Browning said with a frown.

"I'll buy all of your ale for the rest of the day," Grey Cloak offered.

All four of Browning's chair legs hit the floor. He leaned over the table, and out of the side of his mouth, he said, "You got a deal."

13

In a low and dangerous voice, Browning said, "You have to listen to me. We don't talk about the dead. But you need to know. You've earned that. All of you. But keep this between us. Adanadel and Dalsay would have my hide if they knew I'd spoken to you about it." He glanced over his shoulder. "Personally, I don't agree with the silence. I think we should talk about it. But you need to know. Besides, the figurine is lost. It's in the past."

Zora's thigh rubbed against Grey Cloak's as she scooted closer to the table. "Even Tanlin wouldn't tell me about it, and I pestered him repeatedly."

"Tanlin can hold his tongue better than any of us." He emptied his flagon and eyeballed Grey Cloak.

Grey Cloak signaled to the barmaid and pointed at Browning.

"Anyway," Browning continued, "here is what happened. We were on another quest to find a dragon charm. It was me, Adanadel, Dalsay, Tanlin, Tatiana, and her three younger brothers, Jak, Flak, and Tak. Triplets. They were elven warriors with swift feet. Excellent scouts and hunters." He pointed at Grey Cloak. "Something like you but more honest and less sneaky. Well, we'd secured another dragon charm from the Catacombs of Rodham deep in the Shelf. When we made our break, we ran into more trouble.

"A rival group called the Scourge had tracked us to the catacombs. They were after the same thing, a dragon charm. Led by a warrior called Sash and a wizard, Honzur, at the time, the veteran pack outnumbered us five to one. Sash thanked us for doing the 'hard work' for them."

"If your lives were in danger, shouldn't you have given up the dragon charm?" Zora asked.

"Huh. Don't think that we didn't consider it. The problem was, the Scourge are killers. They wouldn't have left us alive, one way or the other," Browning said. "Dalsay assured us of that. But we had an equalizer in the figurine. It had always served us well before, but this time..." His fiery voice lost its strength. "Was different.

"Determined not to lose the dragon charm, Dalsay decided to use the figurine. It had always served us well in the past. We didn't have any reason to worry. Perhaps we'd come to rely on it too much." Browning took a long drink and stared into the distance. "Then black smoke went up, and I saw Honzur's eyes grow big. I tell you, I'd never seen an elf's eyes get so large before. As big as a bugbear's. Then it came." Goose bumps broke out on Browning's forearm.

His fingers tapped the side of his flagon. "I never seen the likes of the creature that formed inside the smoke. It was ghastly. Only about yea tall." He made a space between his hands about three feet. "It had a single eyeball the size of a plate. Tiny horns on its head and a huge mouth filled with razor-sharp teeth. Behind its back, two leathery wings slowly beat, but it hovered more like a humming bird, walking on air. A long tongue uncoiled out of its mouth. It had short muscular arms and a thick, bumpy hide all over it.

"That thing, that impish thing, locked its orb-like eye on Tatiana like a hound eyeballing a pork chop. It said, and I'll never forget it, 'Killsss.' Those bat wings hummed to life, and it whizzed straight for Tatiana. Her brothers rushed in to protect her. They didn't wear much armor, only leather jerkins, and carried longswords and short bows. That thing tore them to ribbons." He shook his head. "The fight looked like a cat in a birdcage having a feast. Its claws tore those boys apart. It would blink and reappear and claw them to death with its talons.

"I tried to help. Adanadel tried to help, and Dalsay too.

But this fiend was too fast, too powerful, too quick. We would swing, and it would blink away in a wink of a lash." He spoke with awe and horror. "I can't say for sure, but that... imp... wanted to kill everything. But it really was bound and determined to kill the elves. For some reason, it hated them and attacked them first. That was when we caught a reprieve. Honzur stood nearby with his fist on his hips. He and his men watched while laughing obnoxiously. It caught that imp's attention, and the imp went after Honzur. That wizard was frightened.

"We didn't stand around to see what happened next. Adanadel and I carried the elves out of there. We found the horses and rode out of the Shelf. We rode for hours and finally stopped to check the brothers. Jak and Flak were dead. Even with Tatiana trying to heal him, Tak couldn't hang on. The wounds they suffered were grave ones. Bloody ones. The sort that you never want to see. We buried them that day."

Grey Cloak had a sinking feeling in the pit of his stomach. Zora's hand was locked on his wrist.

Dyphestive appeared to swallow a lump in his throat and said, "Sorry."

"It was awful. There is no other way of putting it. No one should see a family member killed like that," Browning said. "Especially such a sweet woman as Tatiana. That's why I say mind yourself. Don't ever mention it again. It hurts *me* to talk about it. Imagine how *she* feels. She calls it the Figurine of Horrors, and she has a good reason."

Grey Cloak ran his free hand over his chest and asked the solemn group, "Who are the Scourge, and why are they after the dragon charms?"

14

"It's pretty simple, really," Tanlin said. He appeared behind Browning and startled him mid-drink.

"What is with you people sneaking up on everybody?" Browning asked. "Remind me to sit with my back to the wall from now on, like the rogues guild over there."

In the back corner of the room, a small knot of men and women were quietly talking among themselves. All of them were wearing hooded cloaks and other garments. Grey Cloak wanted to try to listen in on their conversations, but he thought the better of it for the moment.

Tanlin pulled a chair up to the table and sat by Browning. "I overheard you, and I confess, I'm glad you spilled the beans. Don't worry... I won't tell Dalsay." He had a goblet of wine in his hand, and he set it on the table then locked his slender fingers together. "To answer your question, Grey Cloak, the Scourge do what we do but for the opposite purpose. We gather the dragon charms so that more Sky Riders can be trained. They do the same for the Riskers. I'm not supposed to know these things, but I've overheard Dalsay and Adanadel talking plenty."

"So they need the dragon charm so that they can ride the dragons?" Dyphestive asked.

"That's the gist of it," Tanlin said. "According to Dalsay, the Wizard Watch and the Sky Riders work together to build an army of riders to battle Black Frost. Not that we've ever seen it with our own eyes. It is what our faith works us toward. Serving the greater good."

Grey Cloak and Dyphestive exchanged knowing glances.

"What was that?" Zora asked.

"What was what?" Grey Cloak replied.

"That look between the two of you," she said. "You know something, don't you?" She squeezed his wrist. "Spit it out."

Grey Cloak gave her the same story that he'd given before. "We get uneasy when you talk about Black Frost and Dark Mountain. We escaped from their... you know."

"Yes, I know, but there is more to your story than that. I can tell." Her eyes searched his. "What is it?"

"We've seen a Sky Rider," Dyphestive blurted. "Her

name was Anya. She was so beautiful." He smiled dreamily. "I'm going to marry her."

"Oh please," Grey Cloak said. "Quit saying that. And don't tell them everything. They won't believe you."

"We are Talon. They've been honest with us, and we'll be honest with them. It's the right thing to do."

Grey Cloak narrowed his eyes. He didn't like sharing his secrets.

Tanlin and Browning leaned toward Dyphestive.

"You really saw Anya? The Anya?" Tanlin asked.

"Was she alone or with her dragon?" Browning continued.

"She was with Cinder, a magnificent beast with wings that went from one end of this room to the other," Dyphestive said proudly.

"Keep your voice down," Tanlin said. "No need to tell the entire town about it." He eyed Grey Cloak. "I respect your discretion, but when did this happen?"

"Not long before Zora robbed us," Grey Cloak said. "We were leaving the Iron Hills, heading back with our flock."

"And she spoke with you?" Tanlin said.

"We came upon her by chance," he replied. "I snuck up on her, actually." He was lying... she'd snuck up on him.

"And the dragon, Cinder, didn't eat you?" Browning asked.

"No, he was very nice," Dyphestive said.

Browning and Tanlin leaned back and gave each other surprised looks.

"Uh, do you know where she is now?" Tanlin asked.

"No idea. Like I said, it was a chance encounter," Grey Cloak said.

Tanlin rubbed his chin and cheek. "I see, and you never mentioned this to Dalsay?"

"No, and I wouldn't have mentioned it to you." He gave Dyphestive a dirty look. "Some things aren't worth mentioning."

"Oh, I'm certain that Dalsay and Adanadel will want to hear about this," Tanlin said as he stood up from the table. "Immediately."

"They've gone this long without knowing. What will another week or two hurt?" Grey Cloak asked.

Tanlin hustled out of the front door.

"The longer we wait, the madder Dalsay will get," Browning said as he pushed his flagon to the middle of the table. "I need another. And you'll probably need one, too, before Dalsay gets ahold of you." He leaned over the table, facing Dyphestive, and said, "So Anya is something, eh?"

"As pretty as the stars in the heavens," Dyphestive replied.

Browning made his habitual clicking sound, like he was calling a horse, with the side of his mouth. "I wish I could have seen that. An actual Sky Rider. They are titans in this world. Seems to me that the two of you have seen a lot in the few years allotted to you so far."

The barmaid replaced his flagon with a new one and gave him a wink.

"It makes me wonder what else you've seen that you haven't told us yet. Oh well." He lifted his flagon. "Time to drink."

15

ARROWWOOD

Anya the Sky Rider paced through the southern meadows of Arrowwood, a location leagues away from civilization. It was night, and only the stars and the moon were out. Her dragon, Cinder, was lying in the field with his head down in the grasses and his long tail half wrapped around his body. Parts of his scales reflected gold in the bright light of the night sky.

With his eyes closed, Cinder said, "You are killing all of the flowers. Why don't you stop pacing and have a rest, like me."

"Is that all that you want to do? Nap?" she asked. She had her helmet in the crook of her arm, and her plate mail caught the moonlight on the chest. She shined it in Cinder's eyes.

The hard ridges on his brow furrowed, and he sighed,

his toasty breath stirring her long hair. "I really wish that you could relax. It's a wonderful evening. You should take advantage of it."

"We are at war. Now isn't the time to let our guards down." She eyed the sky. High above, a creature soared, circling above her. It began to lower. She put her hand on her longsword and gripped the pommel then pulled the blade halfway free. It was a dragon and a rider just like her. "Cinder, someone is coming."

Cinder opened an eye and turned his head to the side. "That's Firestok."

"Are you sure?" she said.

"I can recognize her from leagues away. She has white underneath her wings. Can't you see?"

Anya squinted. She had excellent vision, but it was no match for a dragon like Cinder. Slowly, the dragon glided downward until Anya saw the white underneath its wings. A rider was on top, armored the same as Anya and dressed in a full open-faced helmet. The tightness in Anya's chest eased as the dragon spread its wings and made a soft landing.

Firestok was a dragon much like Cinder though not as large or rough with ridges. Her ruddy scales were mixed with fiery orange.

A warrior jumped out of the saddle and landed on the ground. With his arms swinging, he marched straight toward Anya, then he took off his helmet and tossed it aside. He was a handsome man with a strong chin, a rugged smile, and wavy gray hair that covered his ears. He opened his arms and said, "Anya!"

She hustled over to his embrace. "Justus!" Then she picked him up and swung him around. "I'm so glad to see you."

"I can see that," he said. Even though he was taller than her, she swung him like a child. "Once again, you've swept me off of my feet. Ho-ho!"

She set him down and gave him another hug. "I really am glad to see you. I haven't seen another human being in weeks."

With his gauntlet-covered hand, he stroked her hair. "I know the feeling." He looked over his shoulder. "How are you, Cinder?"

"I would be better if I were burrowed in a cozy cave somewhere. Otherwise, I couldn't be better," Cinder said.

Firestok waded through the meadow toward Cinder and said, "The older they are, the more they need their precious sleep. It's commonplace with the males, always wanting to rest when work needs to be done."

Cinder lifted his head. "Ah, Firestok, the queen of impolite salutations. It's a pleasure to see you, as always."

He stuck out the horn on his nose, and Firestok bumped it with hers. They nuzzled for a moment.

"I admit, I find your captivating beauty refreshing."

"And I, yours." Firestok showed a smile full of large sharp teeth and batted her eyelashes.

Looking at the sky, Justus said, "It's a beautiful night, isn't it?"

"You sound like Cinder, but yes," Anya replied. "We killed Gustam and Evil Wing."

Justus raised both of his eyebrows and said, "What? Where?"

"In the Iron Hills. We buried them in Crow Valley."

He put his hands on her shoulders and said, "My dear niece, I'm glad you are well. You *are* well, aren't you?"

She nodded. "Yes."

"My goodness, Gustam and Evil Wing, so far south. That's not a good sign at all."

"No, Black Frost is getting bolder in his pursuit of us," she said. "I am certain that there will be more, and I needed to warn you so you can tell the others."

Justus locked his hands behind his back and nodded. "You've done well. Your mother and father would be very proud of you, Anya. I am proud for them. You've grown to be an extraordinary Sky Rider. But don't risk yourself. It's best that we avoid confrontation with the Riskers. Lay low."

"I'm not going to cower."

They started walking through the meadow together.

"And I'm not asking you to," he said. "Stay here, in Arrowwood. Black Frost's dragon forces have an aversion to the elven lands. It's best that we take advantage of that while we build our army. Besides, your encounter with Gustam might have been related to another matter."

She locked her arm in her uncle's and asked, "What do you mean?"

"Our agents in Dark Mountain revealed that Black Frost is searching for two boys, *naturals*, like us, that escaped his clutches. It is believed that they are the children of Olgstern Stronghair and Zanna Paydark."

"Stronghair and Paydark had children together?" she asked, a puzzled look on her face. "Are they part elves?"

"No. Olgstern and Zanna were legendary Sky Riders, our leaders, that Black Frost killed. They had their own families that we thought were also killed. Apparently, Black Frost kept these boys alive to see if they had potential, and if they did, he would turn them into Riskers by corrupting them the same way as other young naturals that he captures."

"It sounds like a stretch," she said.

"True, but apparently, Black Frost wants to make sure that neither of these boys has potential. And if he can't control them, he'll kill them. According to the Wizard Watch, naturals with powerful potential have the ability to even control a dragon as powerful as Black Frost. Imagine if Black Frost controlled such a person. He could control the entire dragon realm. The children of Olgstern and Zanna would have been strong candidates for that."

Anya glanced at Cinder and Firestok. The dragons were

lying beside each other, chirping in their dragon chant. Anya was a natural and had bonded with her dragon, but she didn't have full control over him, only influence. Even if she could control a dragon, she wasn't certain that she would want to. Cinder had a mind of his own, and she respected that. "Shouldn't we be looking for these boys as well?"

"We only recently learned about their escape. Apparently, they slipped Black Frost's grasp a few years ago. The hunt for them has only recently begun, but there is a lot of ground to cover, and boys such as these could have changed a lot in three years. They would be striplings now."

"Do we even know what they look like?" she asked.

"We only have a little information that we snatched from our enemies. The elf is dark haired and has gray eyes. The boy is a big-boned towhead."

Cinder raised his head.

Anya found her dragon's gaze and immediately recognized his knowing look. She turned back toward her uncle and said, "These boys, I think we've seen them."

<h1 style="text-align:center">16</h1>

Anya rehashed the story about her encounter with Grey Cloak and Dyphestive. "They said they were shepherds, but I suspected they were country thieves. The funny thing was that neither one of them flinched when they saw Cinder. I didn't think anything of it at the time. I was more concerned with disposing of Gustam and Evil Wing."

"It seems fate dropped them right into our hands, and we missed it," Justus said as he pulled his arms wide and stretched his back. "Do you think you could find them again? We need to protect them."

"It will be like hunting small prey, but at least we know what we are looking for. Assuming it is them."

"Even if it isn't them, we can't risk ruling out the possibility. We have to find them before Black Frost does." Justus waved his hand at Firestok. "Come on, girl. We need to depart. Our brethren will need word of this."

"Are you going to the Wizard Watch?" Anya asked.

"Yes, the one south of here, below Littleton. The wizards are still gathering dragon charms and helping train more Sky Riders."

"Why do we need the dragon charms?"

"There aren't many naturals left. The dragon talismans allow more people to bond with the dragons." Firestok strolled over the tall grasses, and Justus climbed onto her back. "Without them, we wouldn't be able to field an army at all. But Black Razor has his one agent in the field, pursuing them too. Whoever has the most"—he grabbed the reins and sat upright—"wins."

She nodded.

"What did you say was the name of these striplings?"

"Grey Cloak and Dyphestive."

"That will be helpful. I'll be in touch, Anya. Find them, but be careful." Justus put on his helmet and patted Firestok's long, scaly neck.

She spread her wings, beat them hard, flattening the grasses, and launched herself into the sky.

Justus shouted, "Soar, Firestok! Soar!"

Cinder stood with his head overshadowing Anya and lifted toward the sky. Together, they watched their friends fly away and disappear among the stars.

"It sounds like we have a new mission. I must say, I'm not looking forward to this one."

"Why not? You can spot a varmint from a mile away," Anya said.

"True, but varmints thrive in the woodland. Boys thrive in civilization. And you know how people react when I am spotted."

"Yes, and you love seeing them scatter like rats."

Cinder gave a throaty chuckle. "I do enjoy it. But have you considered that our chance encounter with Gustam and Evil Wing wasn't a chance encounter at all? Perhaps they were closing in on the boys as well, and that was when we came across them."

She put on her helmet and climbed into the saddle. "Hmm, you make a good point. And with Gustam and Evil Wing down, more will follow."

"Need I remind you that Black Frost won't be happy about his brother's, Evil Wings's, demise? He'll send Riskers to avenge him."

"Let them come," she said as she tightened her grip on the reins. "My only regret is that he won't know that I'm the one who did it. Soar, Cinder! Soar!"

Cinder reared up and launched into the sky. With her golden hair flowing from underneath her helmet like a banner, they made a beeline for the Iron Hills.

17

RAVEN CLIFF

L ate in the evening, Drysis and Shamrok entered Raven Cliff. They had donned traveling cloaks that covered their armor, and Shamrok was no longer wearing his crimson skull mask. His rugged face had handsome features, and his hair was very short. He walked half a step behind her.

They took the stairs that led to the entrance of a stone cathedral, and the double doors opened when they arrived on the top landing. Once they were inside, a pair of monks in brown robes closed the doors behind them and hurried away.

In the corners of the cathedral were four soldiers in full armor, standing guard. Rows of wooden pews led all the way to the sanctuary. A man in decorative clothing was sitting in the front pew, and he turned slightly and waved them forward.

"Wait here," Drysis said to Shamrok.

He stood in front of the exit door while glaring at the soldiers standing in the corners, who averted their eyes from his hard stare.

Drysis sat down in the pew behind the man in the front.

He was bald and had a husky build, and he offered his hand and said, "I am Baron Dorenzo. I'm honored to make your acquaintance. I don't believe we've ever hosted Doom Riders in my city. At least not underneath my reign. All hail Black Frost."

She didn't take his hand. "I need you to keep your soldiers out of my business while I am here."

"Consider it done." His hand fell down to his lap. "My eyes have seen the striplings that you are searching for. It appears that one of them robbed a local merchant and spent some time in a jail cell. They have spent time in the Red Claw Tavern as well."

"What is that?" she asked.

"A place where sordid lots frequent. A den for adventurers. As I understand it, these youths have been taken in by a band called Talon. But I don't know the nature of their business. I only know who they are."

"Tell me everything," she said.

"Of course." He cleared his throat. "It would be my honor to be your host at my castle. I realize that you have pressing matters, but I could entertain you with an exquisite dinner. I want to express my appreciation to Black Frost and the fortune he has blessed me with."

"Not interested."

"I see." He dabbed the sweat on his forehead. "Well, this scroll has everything that you need. Where they stay and where they have been over the past few days. I hope it serves you well. And remember, my eyes are your eyes."

She took the scroll, stood up, and walked away.

At the end of the aisle, Shamrok opened the doors. "That was quick."

"Too quick for that bloated windbag." She hurried down the steps and started unrolling the scroll. "Time to snare some urchins."

18

Grey Cloak was lying on his twin bed in the inn, tossing a dagger up and down, and Dyphestive's big frame filled the bed across from him, his boyish face buried in the pillows. The bed bowed in the middle, and his wrist touched the wooden floor.

"I don't know about you, but I'm bored," Grey Cloak said. He flipped the dagger into the ceiling, and the blade dangled. He opened his hand. "Come on down."

"I'm not bored. I'm tired," Dyphestive said. With lazy effort, he glanced at the dagger. "If you don't catch that, you'll have a second belly button."

"Oh, I'll catch it. Don't worry about that. I always catch it, don't I?"

Dyphestive yawned. "Yes."

The dagger fell point first, and Grey Cloak snatched it

by the handle with the tip only a few inches from his belly. "Too easy. It's nice being fast. Very fast."

"If you say so." Dyphestive rolled onto his side. The small bed groaned loudly.

"Goodness, what are your bones made of? Iron?'

"Ha-ha. Aren't you ever tired?"

"No. And normally, you aren't, either."

"Everyone gets tired. Besides, I've been shoeing horses all day."

Grey Cloak rolled his eyes. "We are adventurers now. You don't need to shoe horses."

"I'm not going to sit around and eat and drink like Browning. Have you seen that roll of dough in his belly? He looks like he swallowed a sheep. Don't ever let me drink that much."

"You have to be your own man. I'm not your nanny." Grey Cloak sat up and put his bare feet on the floor and began tossing his dagger up and down again. "Do you know what I was thinking?"

"Oh no. What is it this time?"

"We should form our own company, like Talon."

"What? Why?"

"That's easy. We will be in charge, and we can keep all of the treasure." He flipped the blade over his hand. "Think about it. One adventure, and we could be rich. We could have our own estate, lands, and servants. We could retire."

"We are far too young to retire. Besides, we are a part of Talon. I like Talon."

"I don't. And I don't have any desire to be bossed around by Dalsay or Adanadel. They kept most of the treasure, not to mention the dragon charm. We could also find the dragon charms and sell them to them. Them or the Wizard Watch. I'm certain that they will do business with anybody. Wizards are mysterious people."

Dyphestive threw his pillow at him. "Will you stop it? Can't we stay here and be content? I'm just now getting used to Raven Cliff. I like it. I like our friends, too, and so do you."

"I could live with or without them."

"You like Zora," Dyphestive said playfully.

"She's only one fish in the sea."

"But she's the one that you want to catch."

"Will you listen to me? Hear me out."

Dyphestive nodded.

"We left Dark Mountain because we didn't want any part of the dragon wars. But here we are, matched up with Talon and in the thick of it." He slipped his dagger into his sword belt, which was hanging on his bedpost. "If we keep this up, we'll wind up right back where we started. Dark Mountain. You don't want that, do you?"

"You're speculating."

"Speculating? Where did you hear that?"

"I hear people talking, and I know what words mean."

Dyphestive jabbed a finger at his blood brother. "You're speculating. I say, let things be. Besides, I don't have a problem with us fighting on the right side. At least we are not fighting for the other side. We know what that is."

"We don't need to fight at all. That's my point. There will always be wars, battles, skirmishes, and conflicts." He gave his brother a stern look. "People die because of them, like our parents did."

Dyphestive sat up, his eyes watering. "You don't know that. I don't know that."

"I know what we've been told since we were whisked away to Dark Mountain. I know that it's a lie. They told us that our family was killed at the Battle of Blackstow, but my heart tells me better. It's all lies. The other children might have believed it, but I never did."

Dyphestive pulled his knees up to his chin. "I don't know, but I've always trusted you. Can't we stay? I don't want to starve to death again."

"I'm not saying that we have to leave right away. All I am saying is that we can do what Talon does and have our own gold. Be our own men. Once we have enough chips, we can move on to a place like Monarch City."

Shaking his head, Dyphestive said, "I don't know."

Grey Cloak huffed. "Haven't I always taken care of you?"

"I think it's the other way around. You're the one that gets us into trouble. Besides, how can we go on an adventure? Dalsay is the one that knows where to go. He has the knowledge."

"Yes, and he acquires that knowledge by reading the tomes. We can do the same thing. Every town has records and histories." He scooted to the edge of his bed. "You've seen the men and women in the Red Claw Tavern. Not all of them have a mage among them."

"I don't know. Let me think about it."

"What's to think about?"

"Whether or not I want to follow another one of your stupid ideas or not."

Grey Cloak's mouth hung open. "Stupid? You're calling *me* stupid?" He stuffed his feet into his boots and grabbed his cloak off the hook on the door. "You're the one who is stupid! You towheaded ox!" He opened the door and slammed it behind him.

19

"Grey!" Dyphestive said. "Go ahead, run away. That's all that you do, anyway!" He headed toward the door, stopped, then went back to his bed and sat back down, dropping his face into his hands. "He drives me crazy."

He might have admired Grey Cloak, but he didn't always agree with him. They'd been close as long as he could remember, and Dyphestive would do anything for his brother, but lately, he felt them beginning to separate, and he didn't care for it. It gave him a sinking feeling in the pit of his stomach. He took a deep breath and let out a long sigh. *Maybe I should go after him.*

He made his way over to his window and looked down on the street. It was late at night, and only a few citizens walked the streets, ambling from tavern to tavern or inn to inn. He saw no sign of Grey Cloak.

"Ah, I'll never catch him now." Dyphestive brushed the hair from his eyes and pulled the shutter closed then scanned the small room. He was alone for a change. Even though he felt guilty, he liked it. "Hmm... now I can get some rest without having to listen to his constant talking."

He kneeled down beside his bed and looked underneath it. His iron sword was lying on the floor, and his sack with the anvil inside was beside it. He slid out the anvil and put it underneath his pillow. When his head hit the pillow, he gave a satisfied smile. "My good luck charm."

Dyphestive lay down with his fingers locked against his chest and fell asleep.

Knock. Knock. Knock.

"Who is it?" he mumbled. He was still half asleep when he heard the knocking on the door. He opened his eyes and blinked a few times. *Did I hear that or not?*

Knock. Knock. Knock.

"What did you do, Grey Cloak? Lock yourself out? Pick the lock. You always want to practice." He stuffed his face in his pillow.

Knock. Knock. Knock.

He lifted his head as his sluggish mind came to life. *Maybe it's Zora or Tanlin.* They were the only two members of Talon who had spent any time with him at the inn. He sat up and walked to the door. "I'm coming."

Knock. Knock. Knock.

"I said I'm coming. Zooks!" When he opened the door, he faced a warrior who stood much taller than him and wore a crimson mask. A chill ran down his spine. *Doom Riders!*

The Doom Rider's mailed fist busted Dyphestive in the teeth.

GREY CLOAK WALKED the storefront porches of Raven Cliff with his hands stuffed in his pockets. He skipped away from a giant man who came staggering out of the tavern, and the brute fell face-first in the street. *Reminds me of Dyphestive.*

He would be lying to himself if he didn't admit feeling gravely insulted by his big-boned brother. *He's not even my real brother.*

The fact that Dyphestive had questioned him was what really stung. He'd gotten used to Dyphestive doing whatever he wanted to do, and that was changing.

We never should have joined up with Talon. They are poisoning his mind. And what am I thinking? Zora robbed me not once but twice.

Grey Cloak wrestled with his trust issues as he prowled the streets like a restless tiger. His brother was his best friend, and he didn't like the idea of losing him to someone else. Something always bothered him about other people. All too often, he felt like he could tell when they were lying to him. Deep in his memory, he could see himself as a baby, or a small child, being torn away from his mother's outstretched arms. Not only did he dwell on it, but he could see it in his dreams as well.

He jumped down to the street and circled the blocks. He paid no mind to those who passed him, and they didn't pay him any mind, either. He had much he needed to consider.

Is Dyphestive right? Perhaps we should remain with Talon.

He made a mental checklist and weighed the options. *Zora, good. Dalsay, bad. Adanadel, bad. Browning, bad. Tanlin... hmm... Well, he's a thief, so bad. Tatiana, very beautiful. Fully elven and sharing a bed with Dalsay. Bad. Once again, it seems that my deductive powers are correct. Leave Talon.*

"When I'm right, I'm right, and I know that I'm right," he said as he headed toward Guild Row.

Unlike the streets that hosted many taverns and inns, Guild Row, the busiest place during the day, was very quiet. It was a darker section of town—small lanterns were lit in front of the buildings, and all of the facility doors were locked.

Grey Cloak strolled with the evening breeze in his face. He had the streets all to himself. Not even any soldiers, who normally patrolled the streets, were about. He breathed deeply through his nose as the wind rustled his cloak. *This is more like it. Me, myself, and I. I couldn't ask for better company.*

He wrapped his cloak around his body. The material was soft and warm, and it was light, too, compared to his other cloak, which often weighed him down. He reached inside the lining and pulled a silver chip out then placed it back in the right side of the cloak and pulled it out of the left.

Hmm... what game is Batram playing? Certainly, he knew about this. Or did he make a mistake by giving it to me? He pictured the halfling's impish expression when he gave it to him. And Batram had said something very strange when he left the arcania. He'd said in a devious voice, "It will keep the frost away as well." It was an odd thing to say, but Grey Cloak had shrugged it off because Batram did many odd things.

One thing was for certain—the more he wore the cloak, the more he liked it. He didn't miss the dagger that he'd traded it for at all. Holding the cloak's edges, he flipped them like wings.

Sorry, Batram, you can keep the dagger and the money. I'm keeping this thing.

He started kicking around in his head for more reasons to leave Talon. His biggest problem was with Dalsay. The wizard always seemed to be holding back. They'd gone on a quest to recover a dragon charm, and though they'd found one, what they didn't do was use it on a dragon. There were dragons in the temple, and they didn't even use the charm on them. The ghost had. Talon had left not only the dragons but also the majority of the treasure. *Perhaps I should go back and get the treasure for myself. I could do it without their help.*

Another thing that stuck in his mind was what the hermit had said. *Steal a dragon, save the world.* Those words bounced around in Grey Cloak's head time and again. The problem was, he'd seen his fair share of dragons back in Dark Mountain. He would just as soon live without them.

As he passed a masonry yard, the streets became oddly still. The wind, which had whistled through the rooftops and rattled shutters, had stopped. The sounds of distant voices had died away.

Ahead, he saw another person on foot, coming his way. It was a very tall woman with white hair shining in the moonlight. She was wearing a cloak over her broad shoulders and walked with the gait of a warrior.

Grey Cloak angled away from her path, only to find her veering back into his. He slowed down and looked right at her. She had an eye patch over her left eye and a crossbow strapped over her back. The moonlight showed off her angular but pretty features. But something about her made his skin crawl, and his cloak seemed to tighten over his shoulders.

"Pardon me, elf," the woman said in a distinctive and commanding voice.

He stopped in his tracks, touched his fingers to his chest, and asked, "Me?"

She looked from side to side and said, "I don't see anyone else prowling around here."

"I'm not prowling, only taking a walk." He glanced over his shoulder, hoping that he might see a patrol coming down the road. "Perhaps *you* are prowling."

With her gaze fastened on his, she said, "No, I'm not prowling. But I'm looking for someone. Perhaps you can help me?"

"I doubt that. I haven't been here very long. And I really should be getting back to my parents. They are probably looking for me." He hurried to walk by her.

She deftly stepped into his path and gently laid her hand on his shoulder but held it in a very firm grip. "I'm new to the area as well. Perhaps we can help each other out."

"Listen, lady, if you are trying to rob me, let me be up front about it. I don't have anything. You can search me," he offered as he tried to pull away.

"No, I'm not trying to rob you," she said as she grabbed a handful of his cloak by the front of his collar and lifted him up to his toes. "I only want to ask *you* a couple of questions."

His heart started pumping quickly. Whoever she was, she wouldn't take no for an answer. He noticed that her left arm was covered in chain mail. He managed a feeble smile and said, "As you wish." *I have to get away from her!*

20

Stars in his eyes, Dyphestive stumbled backward, tripped over his own feet, and crashed into his bed. The skull-faced man who had hit him packed a heavy punch.

"Stay down, young fella, or I'll make your night a whole lot worse," the man in the crimson skull mask said. He had a cloak on and was wearing leather armor that had dragon-like scales.

A second warrior entered the room and closed the door behind him. He was dressed the same as the other one, but his ugly skull mask was deep green. "Don't toy with him, Scar. If he's a natural, I wouldn't underestimate him."

"Get the rope ready, Shamrok. He might be a big lad, but he doesn't look to have much fight in him."

Dyphestive's blood chilled. He'd seen Doom Riders before in Dark Mountain. They were the most feared warriors in the north. Only the Riskers were a match for them, and they had dragons. *They finally caught up with us. They'll take us back to Dark Mountain.* His hand locked around the sack that held his small anvil. *No, thanks.*

Scar moved deeper into the room and squatted in a casual manner. He was wearing a belt of daggers and carrying a sword. His forearms were covered in bracers, and his gauntlets looked like dragon paws. He spoke in a rugged voice. "Listen closely, boy. There is an easy way and a hard way. The hard way means I break something. The easy way is that you come along willingly, and I break nothing."

Dyphestive swallowed and said, "I think there is a third option."

"Is that so?" Scar replied. "And what might that be?"

"Watching you... kiss my anvil!" Dyphestive swung the anvil and busted Scar in the face, knocking his mask sideways.

"You didn't see that third option coming, did you, Scar?" Shamrok chortled.

Scar spit a tooth out and said, "Now look what you did, you little upstart."

Dyphestive swung the anvil again.

Scar locked up Dyphestive's arm and shoved him face-first to the floor. "No more of that, lad. Get the rope on him, Shamrok!"

Dyphestive wriggled like a writhing snake and tried to head-butt the Doom Rider in the chin, but Shamrok grabbed one of his arms and started to tie it up, so he tucked his arm underneath his chest.

"He's as strong as a bull," Scar said as he fought to stay on top of Dyphestive. "Be still!" He punched Dyphestive in the back of the head, grabbed his other arm, and tried to pull it backward. "Get that rope around this side, Shamrok. I'm tired of playing."

Together, the Doom Riders started to hog-tie Dyphestive. During the struggle, he thought of his blood brother. *Grey Cloak! I have to warn him!* He pulled his arms underneath his body and tightened up like a clam.

"Bloody horseshoes! The boy thinks he's a turtle. I guess we're going to have to crack that shell. Give him a shot to the ribs," Scar said.

Shamrok kicked Dyphestive in the ribs, but he didn't budge, so the Doom Rider kicked him again. "What is he made of?"

"Kick him harder," Scar ordered.

"I'm kicking him plenty hard, but his big arms are in the way," Shamrok replied.

Scar made an angry grunt. "Help me pick him up."

Together, the Doom Riders lifted Dyphestive—who was balled up like an egg—off the floor.

"Now what?" Shamrok asked.

The Doom Riders shuffled through the room.

Dyphestive cracked an eyelid when Scar said, "We throw him out the window. One. Two. Three." His body swung back and forth. "Heave!"

Dyphestive's body crashed through the window and plummeted to the cobblestone streets.

"ALLOW ME TO INTRODUCE MYSELF. My name is Drysis. And you are?"

"Very uncomfortable," Grey Cloak replied, his feet still dangling. "Would you put me down, please?"

"Only after we have made a proper introduction. I am Drysis. And you are?" she asked again.

"Scared?" Out of the corner of his eye, he saw a horse and a rider coming out of the adjacent alley. Except it wasn't a horse. It was a terrifying beast called a gourn, a horse with the head and scales of a dragon. A man in a blue skull mask was in the saddle. *A Doom Rider!* "Very scared," he uttered.

"You are trying my patience, elf," she replied. She was holding him up by the cloak collar with her left arm. With her right hand, she flipped up the eye patch that covered her left eye, revealing an eyeball that burned like a blue star.

Grey Cloak's body went limp the moment he looked into her hypnotic eye, and he couldn't tear his gaze away from her. His lips silently chewed at the air.

"Now, let's try this gain," the white-haired warrior queen said. "What is your name?"

"Grey Cloak," he said as an invisible force wormed its way deeper into the recesses of his mind.

"No," Drysis said, "your real name."

Despite her powers prompting the true answer out of him, he fought against it. He tried to squeeze his eyes shut. *Don't tell. Don't tell. Don't tell.* But he blurted it out. "Dindae!"

"I thought as much, but I had to be certain. And *Festive* is with you?"

"Yes," he moaned.

Drysis flipped down her eye patch. "Excellent. It appears that I have my elf and, most likely, the other youth as well." Without loosening her grip, she lowered him to the ground.

Grey Cloak sagged as if his life had been sucked out through the marrow of his bones. He wouldn't have been able to stand without her holding him up. Guilt washed over him. He'd betrayed himself and his friend. The Doom Riders had finally caught up with him. Awash with weakness and with a growing headache festering behind his eyes, he said, "What are you going to do with me?"

A riderless gourn walked up behind Drysis from out of

nowhere. Its burning gaze bored into Grey Cloak. Drysis picked him up in her strong arms and laid his limp body over the saddle. She started to tie him down with ropes and said, "We are taking you back to Dark Mountain. Black Frost wants to see you."

21

Dyphestive hit the hard street flat on his chest. He groaned as he rolled onto his back. Scar and Shamrok had shoved their wide shoulders through the window.

"Don't even try to move, boy," Scar said. "Or the gourn will get you."

Shamrok chuckled.

Dyphestive fought his way up to a seated position. He studied the streets. Not a soul was out and about, and he saw no sign of Grey Cloak. When he started to stand, he heard a part growl and part roar and froze, lifting his gaze upward. On the roof, above his room, two gourn with burning stares were looking down on him hungrily. Their clawed toes scratched over the roof, and hot saliva dripped from their mouths and drizzled onto the street between his feet.

Scar hopped out of the second-story window and landed beside him. Shamrok landed on the other side of him. He whistled by using his fingers in his mouth. Both of the gourn vaulted off the roof and landed in the street.

Scar kicked Dyphestive in the gut, and the blow doubled him over, then the gourn hemmed him in. They breathed steamy, sulfuric-smelling air down his face and neck, and fire flickered in the backs of their throats.

"What do you want with me?" he asked.

Scar grabbed him by his hair and pulled his head back. "We don't want you. Black Frost wants you. The sad part is that he wants you alive. Dead would be quicker and easier. Now, don't move, boy, or I'll have the gourn do damage to you that will last a lifetime."

Shamrok began tying Dyphestive's hands up and said, "You don't want that. The gourn's breath will burn your face off, and you'll have nothing but skull like us."

Dyphestive didn't doubt it. He knew about the Doom Riders and the gourn. Their reputation preceded them. Besides, as long as they didn't have Grey Cloak, he didn't care. He was willing to make that sacrifice. *I hope my brother is all right.*

"GREY. PSST! GREY!" Dyphestive said in a hushed voice.

Grey Cloak fought to lift his head in his languid state. His lifeless body was draped over a gourn's saddle, and he was being slow-walked down the streets. "Dyphestive," he said with a thick tongue.

"It's me," Dyphestive replied. "You don't look well."

"That's because I feel like my mind has been turned inside out."

The gourn they were riding on were being led by Doom Riders. Dyphestive was being towed by a man in a crimson mask, and Grey Cloak was tethered by a rider donning a blue skull mask. Drysis and another rider in a green mask were in front of them.

"How are you?" Grey Cloak asked.

"Never better but disappointed that you're in as bad of shape as I am. I was hoping you would escape."

Scar whipped the leather rein over Dyphestive's back. "Don't make me warn you again, boy." He poked a finger at Grey Cloak. "You, either."

Grey Cloak blinked, his eyelids heavy. Drysis's magic eyeball had really drained him but not so much that his natural inclination to escape didn't kick in. He twisted his head around so that he could get a clean look at his brother and mouthed, "Don't worry. I have a plan."

Dyphestive mouthed back, "You'd better use it quick."

Subtly, Grey Cloak began to squirm in his bounds. So

far as he was concerned, no rope or knot could hold him. All he needed to do was get off the gourn and free his hands for a moment. The thought of escaping was another matter. He might be able to run, but Dyphestive would never make it, and the gourn were faster than any horse. At least he could hide, but that wasn't the plan. He needed something else. He was desperate. Twisting left and right, he worked his fingers loose and fell out of the saddle. "Oof!"

The Doom Riders stopped.

"Get him up!" Drysis said. "And secure him better this time, Scar."

"I didn't tie him to the saddle. Shamrok did," Scar replied.

"It wasn't me. It was Blue," Shamrok said smugly.

"Sure, blame the man who doesn't talk." Scar bent down on one knee and pushed Grey Cloak's face into the road. "No more tricks, boy. Do you hear me?"

Grey Cloak gave a feeble nod. With his hands tucked underneath him, he fished something out of his inner pocket. It was the Figurine of Heroes. When Tatiana had thrown it into the woods, he found it, but he didn't tell anybody. Instead, he continued to pretend to look and kept the figurine for himself. He managed a small smile, thinking about it. When Scar hoisted him up and roughly jammed him down on the saddle, he left the figurine on the ground.

Scar grabbed a handful of his hair and said, "Stay put, elf, or you'll be leaking blood for the rest of the trip."

"Leave him alone," Dyphestive said.

"I've heard enough out of the both of you. Drysis, I'm going to gag them," Scar said.

"I beg your pardon?" she said.

"I mean to say, with your permission, I would like to gag them," Scar replied.

"Do as you wish," she replied.

Oh no, Grey Cloak thought. He quickly began recollecting the words that Dalsay had spoken when he last used the figurine. Grey Cloak had a sharp mind and excellent hearing. He started mouthing the words, silently at first, syllable by syllable.

Scar quickly gagged Dyphestive with a cloth and turned on Grey Cloak. "Now it's your turn."

Grey Cloak spoke quickly.

Dalsay's stern voice cut through the night. "Halt!"

Talon had arrived.

Grey Cloak's heart jumped when he saw them. All of them were there—Dalsay, Adanadel, Tatiana, Browning, Tanlin, and Zora.

Dalsay was standing in the front, wearing his midnight-blue robes with arcane silver symbols embroidered in the fabric. The wind picked up and rustled his sleeves. "Leave the youths with us," he demanded.

Drysis scoffed. "Do you know who we are?"

"I do," Dalsay replied. "You are Doom Riders, Black Frost's hunters. The vilest of all peoples."

"Yep, he knows us," Shamrok said.

"And you are Dalsay, of the Wizard Watch," she said. "I know all about Talon, a pitiful band of adventurers that serve the towers." She swung her four-shot crossbow around from her back. "You are no match for the likes of us. Step aside, or we will kill you—all of you."

Both of Dalsay's ring fingers started to glow. "You underestimate us."

"Do I?" She lifted her crossbow to her cheek and took aim at Dalsay. "Let's find out, shall we?" She squeezed the trigger, and a crossbow bolt whizzed by in a silver streak.

A glowing shield of golden energy appeared in front of Dalsay, and the bolt ricocheted off of it.

"Impressive." Drysis pumped the handle underneath her crossbow. The move pulled back the string and rotated another bolt into place. *Clack-clack.* "But can you protect everybody?" She aimed at Adanadel and fired.

The silvery bolt careened straight toward Adanadel's chest. He stood flat-footed. Browning dove in front of Adanadel with his small buckler stretched out. The bolt buried itself in the shield. *Thuk!*

Browning cried, "Argh! The bloody bolt went through my shield and into my hand." He grimaced. "Holy horseshoes, that hurts."

Scar and Shamrok chuckled.

"It sure sounded like it hurt," Shamrok said. "But if you think that hurts, then you don't know what hurt is."

Tatiana rushed over to Browning, and Drysis reloaded another bolt. *Clack-clack.* She fired at Tatiana, and Dalsay moved his shield in front of her. The bolt slipped by the shield and struck Tatiana in the leg. The elven mystic fell to the ground.

Clack-clack. Drysis fired again. That time, she aimed at the exposed Dalsay. He pulled the shield back in front of him in the nick of time. The crossbow bolt blasted right through it and lodged in the wizard's shoulder. Dalsay dropped to a knee.

With skillful grace, Drysis calmly started reloading bolts into her crossbow one by one. "Foolish mage, did you really think your magic could withstand an assault from me?" She patted her quiver of bolts that hung from her gourn's saddle. "Many of my bolts are enchanted, but I like to save those for special occasions. No magic you summon or armor that you wear can stop them."

Grey Cloak's throat tightened as a sense of dread fell over him. When Talon had arrived, hope began to swell, but that feeling had faded. Talon was outmatched by the Doom Riders. The men in skull masks and the woman who led them would kill them without batting an eye.

"Those were only warning shots," Drysis said. "If I have to shoot again, it will be to kill."

"Let us kill them," Scar said as he cracked his knuckles. "I'll take the entire lot of them myself."

"Not if I take them first," Shamrok said. He shed his cloak.

"That sounds like a fair wager. Let's see who kills the most first," Scar added.

Dyphestive gave muffled cries as he tried to spit his gag out.

Tatiana was still on the ground, nursing her leg. Adanadel and Browning made a wall in front of her, and Browning groaned as he pulled the bolt out of his hand.

Dalsay was standing with Tanlin and Zora behind him. His fingers twitched at his sides. His gaze remained locked on Drysis. "Let them go," he demanded again.

"Your demands bore me, Dalsay." Drysis kept her aim on him. "I admire your bravery and your loyalty, however, but my patience thins. Step aside or die. And I mean all of you."

Dalsay shook his head.

"So be it." Without taking her eyes off of Dalsay, she said, "Scar. Shamrok. Go ahead. Have fun."

Grey Cloak watched Shamrok dismount and stroll toward Adanadel and Browning with Scar. They didn't even draw their weapons.

Drysis kept her eyes locked on Dalsay, and she warned him, "Stay out of it. If you so much as flinch or utter a syllable, I will end you."

Adanadel's sword scraped out of his scabbard.

Scar chuckled. "I'll take this one." He was bigger and taller than Adanadel and far more imposing in his dragon-scale armor. "Come on, little man. Let's see what you—"

Adanadel rushed in and swung at Scar's gut. Scar leapt

backward, and the sword tip missed cutting him open by an inch.

Grey Cloak strained his neck as he fought to keep his eyes on the action. *Kill him, Adanadel! Kill him!*

Scar moved like a big cat. When Adanadel attacked, Scar slipped out of the way.

The same action was going on with Browning and Shamrok. The veteran fighter lunged and thrust, only to see Shamrok dance away.

Then like a striking snake, it happened. Scar whisked his sword out of his scabbard, and Shamrok did the same. They launched a fierce assault with razor-sharp blackened steel that sent winded Adanadel and Browning backpedaling. Metal crashed against metal, and the fighters of Talon labored to keep up.

Scar snaked his blade through Adanadel's polished defenses and stabbed him deep in the thigh. Shamrok battered Browning's broadsword and slashed him across the chest.

Adanadel limped as he fought, and Browning parried with two hands, but it wasn't enough.

Scar and Shamrok gored both men straight through the chest.

"*Nooo!*" Grey Cloak screamed. "*Nooo!*"

23

Grey Cloak's initial shock stung like fire. He couldn't believe what had just happened. His friends, Browning and Adanadel, had been cut down. When he glanced at his brother,

Dyphestive's eyes were watering, his brow was knitted, and he was thrashing against the cords holding him fast.

"Don't say that I didn't warn you," Drysis said coolly. "And to think that *I* was trying to be nice." She lifted her shoulders in a little shrug. "Oh well. We might as well kill the rest of them. If we don't, it might come back to bite us."

Scar and Shamrok moved in on Tatiana. Her amulet glowed like fire in her hand, and

Dalsay's right hand charged up with bright-blue fire. He sent a bolt of energy into Scar that sent the man head over heels and skipping over the street and into the porches.

Tatiana's fire swallowed up Shamrok and burned him from head to toe. He raced across the street and dove into a water trough.

Drysis shot the exposed Dalsay in the chest. She pumped the handle on her crossbow. *Clack-clack.* Then she shot him again.

Everything happened so fast. Grey Cloak's survival instincts kicked in. He freed his hands again and slid off of the gourn and into the street. He rolled toward the Figurine of Heroes and said the words of enchantment. "*Osid-ayan-umra-shokrah!*"

The small figurine stood in the street like a piece on a game board.

He repeated the phrase. "*Osid-ayan-umra-shokrah!*"

Nothing happened.

Dalsay spoke inside his head. "*You are missing a syllable.* Osid-ayan-umra-shokrah-ha! *Say it! Throw it between us —quickly!*"

"*Osid-ayan-umra-shokrah-ha!*" He threw the figurine toward Dalsay. It landed between the gravely wounded mage and Drysis and rolled over the street stones and turned upright then began to smoke.

"What trick is this?" Drysis asked with casual amusement. She looked back at Grey Cloak then turned to Ghost. "Secure him and make sure he doesn't slip away again!"

Inky-black smoke spewed out of the figurine and began to take shape. The evening breeze quickly took the smoke away, revealing a part-elf in emerald-and-gold-colored wizard robes. He wasn't very tall, and his hair was long and black and streaked with gray. He had a staff made of white wood with a gemstone nestled in the top. His expression was scholarly and inquisitive.

"Who are you?" Drysis asked.

He kept his face toward her, but the part-elf's eyes darted around as he took in his surroundings and said, "I am Bayzog. I take it that you are not the one who summoned me." He raised an eyebrow. "Strange."

"No, I didn't summon you." Drysis pointed her crossbow at him. "My enemies did in a desperate attempt to save themselves. It seems that will have sealed your doom as well."

Bayzog eyed her with a steady gaze and said, "You reek of evil."

"It would be a sad thing to think that you came all this way to tell me that. Good-bye, Bayzog. Nice meeting you." She squeezed the trigger.

The crossbow bolt exploded into stardust several feet from Bayzog's face. She pumped the crossbow hand and fired again. The bolt turned to water and splashed off of Bayzog's chest.

Drysis clenched her fist and gave an irritated grunt. Shamrok rose out of the trough, and Scar was back on his feet.

She pointed at Bayzog. "Gourn. Doom Riders. Kill him."

The Doom Riders closed in on the part-elf wizard, who stood a little over five feet tall. They were giants compared to him.

Bayzog tapped the bottom of his staff on the road, and the gem in the top glowed with warm blue light. Ice spread from the bottom of the staff and over the street in all directions, covering the road in a second.

The front claws and back hooves of Drysis's gourn scraped over the icy ground, and the beast ran desperately and fell. The other gourn tried to run, only to quickly slip and fall as well.

Ghost, Scar, and Shamrok made their way toward Bayzog on slippery feet, Shamrok using his sword like a cane, but he slipped and fell flat on his back.

Laughter burst out of Scar. "Idiot! Can't you stay on your feet?" He started to skate on his boots toward Bayzog with his sword brandished.

Bayzog twirled his finger, making Scar spin like a top. He sent the brusque man into a collision course with the storefront porches.

From his knees, Ghost used a dagger in each hand to bite into the ice and propel himself forward. He made it within five yards of Bayzog and hurled his blade at the part-elf wizard.

But Bayzog knocked the blade away with a mystic shield on his hand. He blew at the man, and a strong breeze swept through the street and sent Ghost sliding away.

With all of the action taking place, Grey Cloak freed himself from the rope and went to his brother, only to run into a gourn, which snapped at him. He felt something poking in his back, so he looked over his shoulder.

"No, you don't." Drysis was poking the tip of her crossbow bolt into his back. "I've lost all patience with you. Perhaps if I put a hole in your shoulder, you'll stop squirming so much."

"Drysis!" Dalsay called.

Grey Cloak turned toward the voice as well. Dalsay was on his feet with the two bolts still in his chest. Tanlin and Zora were supporting him.

"Leave him alone!" Dalsay said. Lightning danced in his eyes and on his fingers. A bolt of white energy blasted out of his hands.

As quick as a snake, Drysis aimed her crossbow and fired back.

24

The moment Drysis's bolt released, she was knocked from her feet by Dalsay's power. She slid across the ice-covered ground and didn't stop until she hit a wagon wheel.

Dalsay was on the ground with a third bolt in his chest. The white fire in his eyes was dying, but Tanlin and Zora tried to give him aid.

Grey Cloak scurried over to Dyphestive and pulled the gag from his mouth. "I'll get you free."

"No," Dyphestive said with a shake of his bull neck. "You need to run, Grey. Look."

Bayzog's body was starting to fade, the ice on the streets beginning to turn slushy.

Dalsay said in Grey Cloak's mind, *"Take the figurine and go, Grey Cloak. Go. We are with you!"*

"I can't leave you," he said to Dalsay.

"You have to. They are too strong. We can't let them find both of us. Go, brother," Dyphestive pleaded. "Go!"

Grey Cloak looked his brother in the eyes and said, "I'll come for you. I swear it!" He dashed toward Bayzog.

Bayzog's smoky form began to dissipate. "I gave my best. Be brave, young one. Farewell."

The Doom Riders had gathered their legs underneath them and started to close in. Grey Cloak snatched up the figurine and started toward his friends. A quick glimpse revealed the agony on their faces. Adanadel and Browning lay dead on the ground. Tatiana was huddled over them, crying. Tanlin and Zora held Dalsay in their arms.

The wizard's face was ashen. His eyes were weak, and he stared at Grey Cloak and mouthed, "Run."

Drysis's iron-hard voice carried down the streets like a crack of lightning. "Doom Riders, get that elf! Bring him to me!"

"What about the others?" Shamrok hollered back.

"Forget about them. The game is over. They are useless!" She whistled, and her gourn rode back to her spot.

"Go, Grey Cloak. Go," Zora urged with tears in her eyes. "There is nothing you can do for us now."

The Doom Riders went for their mounts, and Grey Cloak took off like a jackrabbit. His feet slipped at first, but in a moment, he accelerated to top speed with the wind whistling through his ears. *Where do I go? I need to hide.*

He raced into an alley and began his dangerous trek through the backstreets. Though he might not be able to outrun the gourn, he hoped he could outwit them. He jumped over boxes and barrels and weaved through stacks of wooden crates then glanced over his shoulder.

No sign of the gourn. He didn't hear them, either, but he kept running as fast and as quietly as he could.

He came to a stop where four alleys intersected. A cat slunk into the darkness, and the stink of refuse settled in. Grey Cloak tried to make a quick decision of where to go. It would be hard to hide from the gourn. They had noses like bloodhounds and no doubt had his scent. He needed to hide where they would least expect it.

When he peered down the other three streets and behind him, he was relieved to see that he'd lost his pursuers, but something wasn't right. *I'm not that fast, am I?*

A soft scuffle of claw on wood caught his ear. He looked up, and his heart jumped.

Ghost was saddled in his gourn on a rooftop two stories high, glowering at him. The gourn's eyes burned with hungry fire.

Grey Cloak bolted down the adjacent alley, and the gourn leapt off of the roof.

Running so fast that his toes barely touched the ground, Grey Cloak sped through narrows with the gourn closing in. Its footsteps became louder, and he could feel its hot breath on his neck.

Ahead, a man opened up the back door of a tavern kitchen. He was smoking a cigar and wearing a greasy apron. The cigar fell out of his mouth the moment he saw Grey Cloak and the gourn closing in.

Moving at full speed, Grey Cloak twisted his hips and juked into the kitchen door. The gourn skidded past the entrance.

Grey Cloak didn't stop to look back. He navigated through the kitchen without rustling a single pot or pan. Two kitchen workers washing didn't notice the breeze he made when he passed. When he burst through the swinging doors behind the bar, he bumped into the back of a rotund bald bartender who stood six feet tall.

"What are you doing, elf?" the lazy-eyed man asked. "Stealing?"

Screams erupted in the kitchen, followed by the loud clatter of iron pots and pans.

"What are you up to?" the bartender asked again as he lunged for Grey Cloak.

"Run!" he warned the bartender. He slipped the big man's clutches and leapt over the bar. "Run!"

The smoke-filled tavern revealed a handful of bleary-eyed patrons. None of them were paying Grey Cloak's disturbance any mind. Many of them were lying with their heads on the table. A few others were staring into their drinks.

Grey Cloak rushed to the window and looked out into the street. He saw two more Doom Riders coming his way. "Zooks." He glanced back at the bar.

The bartender was holding a club in his hand and pushed the swinging door open. "Jumping jugglers!" he cried and fell back.

A Doom Rider burst clear through the wall of wine bottles and racks of hanging tankards behind the bar. The gourn's broad chest crashed straight through the bar, breaking it into splinters. Ghost and the gourn stared Grey Cloak down with burning anger. The patrons scrambled in all directions. Through the window, he could see Scar and Shamrok closing in.

Ghost's gourn blasted out flames like a dragon, which set a man who was scurrying for his life on fire. The man didn't make it three more steps before his body withered like burning wood and his skeleton was covered in ashes.

Grey Cloak's heart beat as quickly as a frightened rabbit's. The Doom Riders had him hemmed in. *What do I do?*

25

When in doubt, run—run like your head's on fire.* If there was one thing that Grey Cloak liked, it was running. But his current problem was whether he could outrun the gourn. They were even faster and more agile than he realized. His fingers flicked open and closed at his sides.

His only way out was a staircase leading up. But he wouldn't make it before the gourn arrived. He stared into Ghost's cold, dead eyes. That Doom Rider, unlike the others, hadn't said a word. He was the kind of terror whose actions spoke for him.

Raising his arms over his head, buying some time while he thought, Grey Cloak said, "I'll give myself up willingly, so long as you aren't going to feed me to the dragon horse."

Ghost gave the slightest nod and grabbed a ring of rope that hung from his saddle.

Fire spewed from the gourn's mouth, crackled, smoked, and spread. The smoke stung Grey Cloak's watering eyes. He peeked through the window. Scar and Shamrok were riding their beasts up onto the porch.

"Get out of my tavern, you skull-faced devil! And take your hound from the netherworld with you!" the bartender said. He pointed a crossbow at Ghost, his meaty arms shaking. "I won't tell you again. I've been around. Get out!"

Ghost didn't turn his haunting stare away from Grey Cloak. He tossed the rope on the floor toward him.

"I warned you," the bartender said. He squeezed the trigger. The crossbow bolt hit the gourn in his right flank, and the dragon beast reared. Its clawed feet came down hard and cracked the floor planks. Rider and beast turned on the foolish man.

Grey Cloak dashed for the steps and went up the entire staircase in two lengthy strides. Then he flew down the hallway and raced toward the closed glass window at the end. He turned to look over his shoulder, and the Doom Rider was cresting the stairs. The warrior and the beast chased Grey Cloak, their big bodies filling the cramped hallway. Though Ghost was stooped in the saddle, his head crashed through a small chandelier. The gourn knocked paintings off the walls and ripped up the carpet with its clawed feet.

Face-first, Grey Cloak dove through the glass window-pane. He sailed across the alley and through a glass window of another building and rolled across the floor. He was in a closed tavern. The chairs were on the top of the tables.

His face and hands were filled with small shards of glass. "Gah!" He ran to the other side of the room, jumped over the bar, and headed into the kitchen. Then he jetted through the back door into another alley.

The sounds of the Doom Rider running roughshod through the tavern reached him. The hunter was hot on his tail. *I have to shake them. Think, Grey Cloak. Think!*

He was a dead elf in open spaces. He had to go where they couldn't reach him. Rats scurried across the street then vanished into the grate that led into the sewers. *That's it!*

Grey Cloak stopped over a storm drain grate, hooked his fingers around the nasty metal, and pulled. But the grate didn't budge.

Ghost entered the alley, no more than thirty yards away. The gourn made a frightening roar.

The muscles in his arms knotting, Grey Cloak put his back into it, but the storm drain held fast. "What are you? Anchor to the world? Urk!"

The gourn came at him with its head low, moving at a slow pace.

Behind Grey Cloak, another gourn roared. Scar and Shamrok rode into the alley at the opposite end.

Grey Cloak caught a glimpse of his brother, and their eyes met.

"Run!" Dyphestive screamed. "Run!"

Grey Cloak pulled with all of his might, but his strong hands slipped free, and his back hit the wall. *I'm useless. If I only had Dyphestive's strength.*

"It looks like we finally cornered the little rodent," Shamrok said in a cocky tone. "Now we can finally get something to eat. Be still, varmint."

Hands on his knees, Grey Cloak panted. He'd never run so hard before. Then he noticed a hasp on the grate that was covered in grime, and he scraped the grit away with his fingers and peeled the corroded latch open. When he flipped the grate open, it slammed on the ground with a loud *bang*.

"Don't you dare, you little jackrabbit!" Shamrok yelled.

Ghost spurred his gourn forward.

"No jackrabbit for you today, scary face!" He saluted and jumped into the hole, then he belly-crawled as fast as he could. "I'll come for you, Dyphestive!" His words echoed down the narrow tunnel. "I swear it!"

A gourn stuck its nose in the mouth of the storm drain then let out a jarring roar and released its flames. Hellish fires licked at Grey Cloak's boots. The suffocating heat took away his breath, and the sludge and grime dried up all around him. Using his elbows, he pressed on, through the rats, webs, and grit.

He didn't stop until he could no longer go on. Deep below the streets of Raven Cliff, he huddled in a corner and shivered. He had goose bumps all over him. Above, people were shouting. Drysis was barking angry orders.

Grey Cloak smirked. *Her being mad makes me happy.* He pinched his nose. *I need to get out of this stink.* He summoned his energy reserves, and on shaky limbs, he crawled away from the sounds of Doom Riders and their demonic horses.

26

D rysis gathered the Doom Riders on the street closest to the last place they'd last seen Grey Cloak. She gritted her teeth and stared down her men then pointed the tip of her reloaded crossbow at all of them one by one and said, "You... you... and you failed me! He's one elf against the fastest beasts on all fours, and you lost him."

Scar lifted his skull mask, revealing many battle scars. Some of the wounds were deep and ugly, with an irritated redness that never healed. "No disrespect, fearless leader, but that elf doesn't move like an ordinary elf. You saw that."

Lowering the crossbow on Scar, she answered, "I saw the same as you did, but you don't hear me making excuses, do you?"

"Of course not, but this boy is a natural. It's no surprise

that he slipped us at the moment, but we'll find him. You know that we will."

"You'll never find him," Dyphestive interjected. "No one has ever caught him when he didn't want to be found. You might as well consider him gone forever." He sniggered.

"Seal his jaws, will you?" Shamrok asked Scar. His gourn had its nose in another storm grate. It sniffed and snorted loudly, its sharp claws scratching at the road. "My gourn still has the scent."

Scar twisted around in his saddle and pulled a dagger from his sword belt. "It's time to close those gums of yours, boy." He bopped Dyphestive in the back of the head with the butt of his dagger.

Bright spots exploded in Dyphestive's eyes. He shook his thick neck and said, "I'm still awake. Heh-heh. Why does your face look like rawhide? Did you lose a fight to a horsewhip?"

"Funny, boy. Real funny." Scar hit Dyphestive in the same spot but harder.

"Rawhide!" Dyphestive shouted back.

Scar struck him again. "What is your skull made of? Iron?" He hit him again.

"Rawhide!" Dyphestive yelled.

"I'm going to turn you into rawhide!" Scar shouted. He flipped the blade around in his hand and aimed it point first at Dyphestive.

"Stop it!" Drysis ordered. "Scar, we can't kill him. And

we aren't here to punish him." She shook her head. "Do the wise thing and gag him."

"As you wish." Scar stuffed his dagger back into his belt then pulled his mask back down and dismounted. Using a strip of cloth, he gagged Dyphestive. Then he lifted Dyphestive's head by a handful of hair, jabbed a finger at his nose, and said, "Boy, it's a long trip, and you don't want to make me any madder than you've made me."

Dyphestive offered a muffled "Rawhide!" and went silent. He was glad that Grey Cloak had gotten away and only wanted to distract his enemies. *Go, Grey. Get far away. I'm borrowing all of the time that I can.*

"Shamrok. Ghost," Drysis said as she shouldered her crossbow. "Do you both have the stripling's scent?"

"Aye," Shamrok offered.

Ghost nodded.

"Let us proceed quietly, shall we? He can't stay in the sewers for long. If the stench doesn't kill him, then the sewer wolves will."

Dyphestive's head rose. *Sewer wolves? What are those things?*

Scar gave a sinister chuckle. "Heh, I forgot about those things. Once they get ahold of the elf, he'll look a lot worse than me."

THE DRAINAGE PIPE opened up into a larger wash that was almost tall enough for Grey Cloak to stand in. He crouched down as he made his way through the dark tunnel. His keen eyes could barely make out the outlines of the walls, but the grates in the city streets offered enough light for him to quickly make his way through.

Grey Cloak kept to the wall, to the side of the murky waters, which trickled by his feet. He kept going, increasing his distance from his enemies. All the time, his mind was racing.

Dalsay, Adanadel, and Browning were dead. The rest of Talon could be dead, as well, for all he knew. And Dyphestive was a prisoner. *This is my fault!*

Even though he was young, he'd always thought of himself as more than capable of handling anything. When they escaped from Dark Mountain, he figured he would be free, or at least he hoped. But in the back of his mind, he always felt that the sands of the hourglass would run out— that his past, and Dyphestive's as well, would catch up with them. It had, and not only had it cost him, it had the lives of so many others too. *I'm a fool. I never should have gotten involved in all of this. I should have moved to the Shelf and lived like a hermit.*

Grey Cloak snaked through the tunnels, careful to keep his hands away from the rotting muck and grime on the walls. His footfalls were quiet, and the streets above were silent. He moved with his eyes on the grates that he passed, watching for moving shadows. *I don't hear them, but I know they are out there. Watching. Waiting.*

He drew his cloak around his shoulders and breezed through the stink like a shadow, his quick and quiet footsteps taking him from one tunnel intersection to another. He hoped to make it to the cliffs, where the waters drained into sludge pools. He'd seen them before from the south side of the city.

Zooks. That's exactly where they'll look for me to come out. Should I go or turn back? He turned around and began to double back. Then came the sound of feet splashing in the dark waters. He narrowed his eyes. Something was coming his way.

The nighttime light shone through the grates on wolflike hounds padding through the drains. They were moving in a pack, at least four of them. Their eyes flickered like bloodred gems, and their lips curled back over their fangs, hungry growls escaping their black lips.

"Nice doggies," he said politely as he backed up.

The lead sewer wolf jumped forward, and the pack raced behind him. Grey Cloak turned tail and ran like the wind.

27

The tunnel narrowed then opened to the bright night sky. Grey Cloak skidded to a stop, his toes hanging just over the edge of a cliff. Hundreds of feet down were a sludge pool and a waterfall of murky water splashing off jagged rocks. Behind him, the sewer wolves raced down the cramped tunnel with their heads low and jaws snapping.

Grey Cloak's fingers reached outward and found purchase on the cliff face rock, and he started pulling himself out of the tunnel. Then the lead wolf bit at his leg, and its teeth sank into the heel of his boot.

He clung to the cliff face with all of his strength. The wolf dangled from his boot, its powerful jaws locked on the leather. The other dogs stuck their heads out of the tunnel and barked at Grey Cloak with slavering mouths.

"Get off of me, hound!" Grey Cloak said. He started

wiggling his foot inside his boot, and his fingers began to slip from the small lip of rock. Using his free foot, he tried to push his other boot off. He could hold himself, but he couldn't hold himself and a thrashing wolf that was a moment from jerking them both down to their doom.

The wolves in the tunnel barked louder.

"Will you *stop that*?" He looked up—only ten feet between him and street level. The boardwalks and stairs that led up and down the cliffs were much farther down. Nothing else was beneath him. "I don't want the Doom Riders to know where I am."

The wolf latched onto his boot jerked hard, and his fingers pulled away from the ledge. Down he went. His toes clipped another ledge below him, slowing his fall, and he caught the lower ledge with his elbow and hands. The stiff landing jarred his body. The sewer wolf and his boot wrenched away from his foot, and they plummeted to the rocks and the sludge pool.

Grey Cloak winced at the wolf's impact. "Better it than me." He started to climb on shaky arms while the other wolves barked at him. He growled back at them. "Filthy beasts. Go back inside your sewer."

Hand over hand, he made it to the top and pulled himself underneath the railing and onto the street, which was clear to the east and the west. West led back toward the decks that led down to the valley.

Maybe I can hide in the Red Claw Tavern.

He sucked through his teeth. That was when he noticed shards of glass in his hands. He gingerly picked them out then hobbled east, away from where he'd encountered the Doom Riders. He walked funny with his left boot missing.

A shame. I liked these boots. They were the best that I ever owned. But I'm faster without them. I need to hide and figure this all out.

Grey Cloak pulled his boot off and tucked it under his arm. He continued moving quickly along the railing that overlooked the cliffs, checking over his shoulder from time to time. *Where to go. Where to go. Where to go. Maybe I could hide at Batram's. Perhaps he can help me.*

He glanced behind him. All four Doom Riders were following him, though they were many yards away. *Holy horseshoes! Where'd they come from?*

The Doom Riders were spread out thirty yards, filling the street between the cliffs and the front buildings. The only ways Grey Cloak could go were east or over the cliff's railings. He would never make it back into the streets. The Doom Riders would cut him off. He backpedaled east, away from them.

"Give it up, Dindae," Drysis said. She was leading from the middle, moving at a slow pace, with Shamrok to her right by the railing and Scar and Ghost to her left. "There is nowhere else left for you to go."

He fanned his boot in the air and said, "Do you happen to know where I can find a cobbler at this late hour? I lost a boot on account of your pursuit, but if you leave me alone, I won't charge you for it."

"You're a funny elf," she said. "But I don't like funny. Now, you will return home, fulfill your destiny, and become a Risker. I can't imagine why any child would want to avoid that station."

"First, I'm not a child. Second, it's my life, and I'll be the one to determine what I say and do."

"This boy has a mouth on him," Shamrok said. "If you ask me, Black Frost would be better off letting us kill the both of them. They've been nothing but trouble so far, and methinks that will only continue."

"That's not for us to decide. We serve. We execute," Drysis said.

"Perhaps we could tell Black Frost that they died in an accident," Scar suggested.

She gave Scar a frosty look. "No more suggestions." She returned her stare to Grey Cloak. "You are tired and wounded. You've run out of exits. You need to come with us, *Grey Cloak.*"

"Ah, I see what you are doing," he replied. "You're trying to win me over, gain my trust, but that's not going to happen." He took a quick look behind him. He was approaching a place called Lovers' Gorge, a nook in the cliffs that angled toward the city. A bridge crossed the gap near the stores. He wouldn't be able to make it to the bridge, but he thought he might be able to jump the gorge.

"I'm not going back there." He threw his boot at her. "Not alive, that is!"

Grey Cloak sprinted toward Lovers' Gorge. A metal railing was in front of the edge. He would have to jump it too. *I can make it! I can make it!* He hurdled the railing, sailed over the gorge, and soared halfway across. *This is much wider than I thought it was.* He started to descend with five yards left to the other side. *I can't make it! I can't make it! Dragons of mercy, I can't make it!*

28

Dyphestive watched in horror as his brother sailed over the railing and vanished into the gorge. *No. No. This can't be happening.*

"That elf is insane," Scar said as he led his gourn toward the railing.

"Unbelievable," Drysis muttered.

The Doom Riders and their mounts hung their heads over the railing and peered into the gorge.

Dyphestive squirmed the best he could to try to see what was going on. *Be alive! Be alive! Be alive!*

"There he is!" Shamrok pointed downward. "That's a long way down, and he isn't moving. No one could survive that fall. That's five hundred feet down. Too bad for him."

"Do you want me to climb down and fetch the body?" Scar offered. "Glad to do it, but it might be mushy."

Drysis gave an aggravated sigh. "This isn't how I planned this. We should have captured him. We failed." Her knuckles cracked when she clenched her fist. "We'll wait. Make sure he's dead. The carrion eaters can feast on him after that."

"You have to admit, that was quite a jump," Shamrok said. "It looked to me as if he almost made it."

"Aye," Scar said. "I would have made it."

"Twenty gold chips says that you can't," Shamrok offered.

"I'll take that bet. But I get to do it on my gourn."

"No," Shamrok said.

"Idiots. Wind your necks in. Your chronic musings make my ears ache." Drysis looked at Dyphestive. "It's going to be a long road for you now that your friend is gone. I sternly suggest that you behave yourself from here on out. But don't worry—I won't let you wind up like him. Don't even think about it. You're going back to Dark Mountain, alive, one way or the other."

29

"It's an interesting place," Lythlenion said as he clawed his orc fingers through the white hairs of his beard. Two men with wheelbarrows loaded with stone hustled by him and Rhonna. "A busy place." He sniffed. "Smells good too."

Rhonna grunted. They'd arrived in Raven Cliff from the north in the wee hours of the morning. The gnawing in her gut hadn't stopped since Lythlenion showed the messages of Grey Cloak and Dyphestive being in danger. "We aren't here to sample the local cuisine."

"I know, but seeing how we are in the area, and it is breakfast time, perhaps, well, we can stop for a bite," he suggested politely.

"No," she replied in her usual gruff manner.

Lythlenion slid in front of her and walked backward. "You know that we can't walk the streets of a foreign city and expect the whereabouts of your friends to slap us in the face. We need to blend in with the locals, listen, and ask, well, a few questions." He offered a warm smile. "Over breakfast perhaps."

Rhonna's brow knitted, but she continued her quick march through the city.

"Come now, you know that you are hungry. Even for a dwarf, you have to be."

"Fine. Pick a spot, but make it quick," she said. "Anything to stop your yapping."

He wrung his hands and said, "Oh, thank you, thank you, thank you." Then he zeroed in on an outdoor café where an elven cook was working over a coal-burning griddle. He pulled a chair out for Rhonna, and they took a seat underneath a canopy. He inhaled deeply through his nostrils. "This is wonderful. Thank you."

Rhonna nodded.

Lythlenion ordered an omelet and hot biscuit cakes for each of them, and the server gave them each a goblet of fruit juice.

Staring at the liquid, Rhonna asked, "What is this?"

"Squeezed juice. Isn't it delicious?"

"No." She shoved her metal goblet over to him. "Remind me never to take you to Dwarf Skull. It would be embarrassing."

"A little elven culture would never hurt anybody. The elves make excellent food. I never miss anytime I sample it."

"Are you sure you are an orc? You sound like you are part elf to me."

"Possibly on a great-great-great-great-great-grandmother's side." He flagged down the elven server. "My friend prefers another refreshment."

"Ah," the male waiter said politely as he glanced at Rhonna. "Our founders make an excellent breakfast stout."

"Is it dark?" she asked.

"Our darkest."

She nodded.

The server returned later with a tankard of breakfast stout and his arms loaded with steaming food. He deftly placed the large metal plates on the table. "Enjoy."

Each plate had an omelet stuffed with assorted cheeses, sautéed vegetables, and grilled meat. The omelets sat on plate-sized flat biscuits smothered in buttery sauce.

Lythlenion tucked a cloth napkin into his collar and picked up his fork and knife in his hairy mitts. "This is going to be good."

Rhonna remained tight-lipped. She couldn't have cared less about the food. It was the ale that she wanted to sample. She took a drink. It was good—very good. It almost forced a smile.

"How is your ale?" he asked.

"I've had better." She drank it down, flagged down the server, and said, "I'll have another."

30

It wasn't long before the conversations between the locals caused Rhonna's ears to perk up. They were chattering about Doom Riders chasing someone down in the city. Most of the people dismissed the stories as a rumor, but not all. One man heard it from another man who heard it from another man who heard it from a dwarf.

Rhonna and Lythlenion finished gobbling up their food, asked a few questions, and tracked the dwarf down. He worked at a nursery, where he chiseled out stone statues for people's gardens. He was working outside, chiseling away at a three-foot-tall hunk of white marble that was taking the shape of a dragon. The dwarf had short, powerful arms and wore no sleeves, and his brown hair and beard covered most of his face and chest.

"Are you Doosk?" Rhonna asked.

"Aye," Doosk said without looking at her.

"I'm Rhonna, from Havenstock, and this is Lythlenion from Harbor Lake. We heard that you witnessed Doom Riders a few nights ago. Will you tell us about that?"

Doosk set his chisel and hammer down, dusted off his stubby fingers on his overalls, pulled up a stool, and sat down. "I saw 'em. Four in all. They chased down striplings. A man and an elf. There was a nasty scrap over from Guild Row. I was night walking. Collecting. Folks drop all sorts of things as they hustle all day with holes in their pockets. I saw those riders. Ducked into the shadows. Couldn't keep my eyes off of it."

"What happened? Where are they?" she asked.

"I tell you what happened. Bad happened." Doosk wiggled his bushy eyebrows. "Those striplings had allies. Their blood is on the stones. A sad thing."

Rhonna and Lythlenion exchanged glances. "What about the youths?"

"I should have asked to begin with, but what interest are they to you?"

She was straightforward with Doosk. "I'm a friend. I raised them for the past three years. They ran away, and I've been looking for them since the Doom Riders paid me a visit."

Doosk scratched the side of his beard and nodded. "Doom Riders. Everything they say about them is true. The big one, the blonde, they towed him away, north. I saw it with my own eyes because I followed after them. The elf, well, I fear to say, but he perished when they chased him into the gorge. He almost made the jump. I thought he had it." He gave a sad nod. "I wanted to help, but I'm a sculptor not a fighter. Sorry about your friend."

Rhonna's eyes watered, and it felt as if her heart flipped inside out. Lythlenion placed a hand on her shoulder.

"Sorry, Rhonna." Lythlenion cleared his throat and asked, "Do you know anything else about these other people who helped them?"

"Talon," Doosk replied. "They are part of a group called Talon. I heard the evil lady say it."

"Drysis," Rhonna said in a bitter voice. She nodded at Doosk. "Thank you for the assistance."

Doosk picked up his hammer and chisel and spun them in is fingers. "If you need a headstone for a grave, let me know. I would be happy to help you out. Sorry about your friends. Sounds like they must have been mixed up in something awful."

RHONNA WAS STANDING on the bloodstained road. Her chubby fingers were interlocked, and her thumbs were rolling over each other. "What do you think?"

"I think we need to ask more questions," Lythlenion said. He was kneeling over another spot. A bouquet of flowers was covering the blood, and the leaves were wilting. "Somebody cared. I know that we've seen our share of battles, but knowing someone was killed in cold blood makes my heart ache."

"It was a fight. Whoever these fellas were, they knew what they were doing." She rubbed her jaw. "The strange thing is that the city patrol doesn't know a thing about this." She'd asked a group of soldiers that she encountered earlier. None of them knew a thing.

"Where do we go now?"

"We need to figure out who Talon is. They'll have answers." She tilted her head toward a tavern. "Come on. I'll buy you something to eat."

"Really?"

They took a spot at a window inside a musty tavern. It was late in the day, and already, many of the hard-working laborers were filing in from the heat and beginning to unwind inside the shady tavern. She and Lythlenion sat on a tall stool with a clear view of the street. She didn't take her eyes off of the battle-marked spot on the road.

Lythlenion dipped a wooden ladle into a big bowl of stew. "This doesn't have the same flavor the elven tavern offers. No spices, not even salt and pepper in this." He smacked his lips and pushed it away. "Perhaps I'm getting spoiled."

"Is it better than your wife's cooking?" she asked without taking her gaze off of the road.

"A fair point." He pulled the bowl back. "I should appreciate it... and your generosity, and ignore my spoiled palate." He dug in. "So are we waiting here, or did you have something else in mind?"

"I have a plan."

He nodded. "Should I ask?"

"I'm curious to see if anyone else shows up and leaves more flowers. We'll give it a while."

"Coming from a dwarf, that could be hours or even days."

"Uh-huh," she said absentmindedly. Rhonna was torn inside. She wanted to go after Dyphestive, but they would never be able to catch up to Doom Riders with a two-day lead. She didn't have any desire to face Drysis, either. The evil woman had proved that she was a merciless killer. In the meantime, however, Rhonna would find out what happened to Grey Cloak. She wouldn't believe he was dead unless she saw it with her own eyes. *He's too hardheaded to die so easily.*

Hours passed, then a part-elven woman wearing a nice burgundy traveler's cloak stopped at the spot on the blood-stained road and glanced over her shoulder. She pulled a bouquet of flowers from underneath her robes and replaced the dead ones. Then she bowed her head and hurried away.

Rhonna knocked Lythlenion's hand out from underneath his chin. He'd been dozing. "Come on. Let's go."

31

Rhonna and Lythlenion followed the part-elf woman back to a tailor shop. Inside were racks of assorted clothing for men and women along with shelves of folded clothing. A skinny man in trousers and a long-sleeve dress shirt was standing behind the counter at the front door. His hair was neatly combed, but his eyes looked tired.

"Good evening," the man said as he folded up a shirt. "Welcome to Tanlin's Fine Fittings. I'm Tanlin. We were just about to close for the day, but I'm more than glad to help you as long as you like."

Rhonna nodded.

"Thank you," Lythlenion said as he ran his hands through a rack of colorful dresses. "I was looking for something for my wife."

"I see. Well, fittings for dwarves are in the far left corner." Tanlin pointed to the shelves in the back. "It's robes. We've never fit a dwarf in a dress. But we can."

Lythlenion tossed his head back and let out a hearty laugh. He slapped his hand on Rhonna's shoulder. "No, she isn't my wife. My friend, yes, but not my wife. My wife is human. Nicely built." He shaped a figure in the air with his hands. "And very beautiful."

Tanlin gave a friendly laugh and said, "My mistake. But this dwarven lady is a beauty in her own right."

Rhonna arched an eyebrow and said, "You haven't seen many dwarven women, have you?"

"Er, well, no."

"Thought so." She waded deeper into the store, searching for the part-elf that she'd seen coming in. Her hand caressed the soft clothing. She'd gotten used to sleeping underneath a burlap blanket for decades and not wearing much more than a blacksmith's heavy-stitched overalls. The thought of comfort escaped her, but the soft cotton fabric aroused her curiosity.

As Lythlenion moseyed through the store, talking nonstop to Tanlin, Rhonna made her way to the back of the building. A curtain was between the shelves, and she pulled it aside, revealing a passage to the back. She started that way.

"Can I help you?"

Rhonna spun on her heel and pulled a knife. "Jumping

jackrabbits. Where'd you come from?" She was facing the young woman she'd seen in the street.

The young woman replied coolly, "I must have been buried in the dresses. I work quietly." She eyed the knife in Rhonna's hand. "It wouldn't be the first time I spooked a customer. Sorry."

Rhonna slid her knife into her sheath and said, "Not a problem."

"I'm Zora." She offered her hand and a smile.

"Uh, Rhonna."

"Can I help you find something?"

"No, my friend is looking. I don't put much thought into my clothing."

"I can see that," Zora quipped, "but that doesn't mean that we can't fit you into something more... clean and comfortable?"

"Listen, little sister, I'm a blacksmith. Not some high-brow teetotaler. It's my friend that is looking."

Zora turned her lovely face toward the front, where Tanlin and Lythlenion were in an excited conversation. "Ah, I see that your friend and Tanlin are very engaged. That's a good thing. Tanlin has had a rough couple of days."

"Why's that?"

"He... well, we lost some friends. It was sudden. It will be a long time before we get over it." Zora brushed her auburn hair over her shoulder, and her chin quivered for a moment. "I'm sorry. I shouldn't burden you."

"Listen, I'm not one to beat around the bush, so does this have something to do with..." She lowered her voice. "The Doom Riders?"

Zora's eyes widened then narrowed. "What do you mean?"

"I saw you leave flowers on that spot in the road. We followed you."

"Why? What business is it of yours?" Zora started to tear up.

"My name is Rhonna. I'm a friend of Grey Cloak and Dyphestive... sort of."

Zora caught Tanlin's eye and said, "Close the store!" As soon as he did, she burst out crying.

32

Hunger. Anger. They defined Dyphestive's existence as he was towed along behind Scar's gourn. They were far north, approaching the high peaks of the border mountains of Ugrad. He'd seen those stark peaks before, when he and Grey Cloak made their escape from Dark Mountain. He'd never wanted to see them again.

Ghost was riding behind him. The Doom Rider never said a word. Drysis and Shamrok were paired up in the lead.

The group rested very little. They walked all day long, and sometimes Dyphestive rode on a gourn, doubled up with Scar. It made for a very uncomfortable situation.

Scar had killed Adanadel. Shamrok had slain Browning. Drysis had murdered Dalsay.

For all that Dyphestive knew, the rest of Talon might

have been killed, but he didn't think so. The only other certainty was that Grey Cloak, his best friend and blood brother, the only family he'd ever known, was gone.

He shuffled along on heavy feet with his head hung low. Though he wanted to run, he knew they would catch him. He wanted to fight, but he was clearly outmatched. He'd lost, and he was going back, and no matter how much he dreaded it, he had no way of escaping.

The company picked up the pace over the rugged and dusty path. Scar spurred his mount forward. The rope tied to the gourn's saddle horn tightened and jerked Dyphestive clear off of his feet, and he hit the ground belly first. He spit dust from his mouth.

Scar laughed and dragged him. "What's the matter, boy? Can't you keep up?" He pulled off his mask and drank from a bloated waterskin, then he shook it, making the water slosh. "I bet you're thirsty too."

"No," Dyphestive muttered. He spit dirt out of his mouth again. His lips were dry and cracked. The Doom Riders had made it clear that they weren't going to make it easy on him.

Scar guzzled down another long drink of water. With the sun highlighting his marred face, he let out a refreshed "Aaah!"

Dyphestive wasn't one to hate, but he hated Scar. At least, he did more than the rest. He shifted into a sitting position.

"Get up, boy," Scar said as he watched Ghost trot by. "We need to catch up with the rest. You're slowing us down."

The one saving grace that Dyphestive had was that he still had his boots on. They were made of hard leather and had a sturdy sole. When Scar turned his back and started to ride forward, Dyphestive set his heels against a rock that jutted up from the hard-packed ground. He wound the rope around his immense hands and held tight. The slack in the rope began to tighten.

Dyphestive clenched his jaw, and his brow furrowed. He summoned all of the strength in his legs, arms, and back and tugged the rope with all his might. The power he let loose pulled the gourn up by the saddle horn.

The dragon beast reared and gave a startled roar. Dyphestive kept pulling. The gourn reared again.

Scar fell out of the saddle. "Whoa!"

Dyphestive pulled the gourn backward. It crashed onto its back and wiggled to get back up. He charged Scar, who was lying on the ground, fighting to bounce back up. Dyphestive tackled the man and plowed him into the ground, knocking the wind out of Scar with an audible "Oof." With the man off balance, Dyphestive wrapped the rope around his neck.

Scar gave a desperate "Urk!" and his fingers clawed at the rope.

Dyphestive was latched on to the man like a giant tick

and pulled tighter. He wasn't a killer, but something came over him, and he really wanted to kill the man. He threw his head back and groaned. "Aaargh!"

Suddenly, Scar pulled a dagger from his belt and slashed Dyphestive across his fingers.

But Dyphestive held on. The rest of the Doom Riders gathered around him. Drysis held her hand up to hold them back as she watched with avid interest. Dyphestive yanked the rope again.

Scar's razor-sharp knife sawed through the rope constricting his neck, and he tore away from Dyphestive's mighty grip and gasped for air. He was on his hands and knees. Blood dripped from the self-inflicted wound on his neck. He glared at Dyphestive. "I'm going to kill you, boy!" He lifted his dagger and charged.

"Stop!" Drysis commanded.

Scar froze in his tracks. His body trembled, and his face was red with rage. Through clenched teeth, he said, "He needs to die, Commander."

"That is for Black Frost to decide. Not you," she said. "Put the blade away, Scar. The youth got the best of you. You're going to have to live with it."

Shamrok gave a raspy chuckle.

Scar pointed the tip of his blade at Dyphestive and said, "I'm going to make you suffer one way or the other." He jammed his dagger back into his sheath. "I swear it."

Dyphestive held his bleeding fingers, and his chest

heaved. His strength was sapped. He had no doubt that Scar would make him pay, but it was worth it.

Scar tied a bandana around his neck. His gourn rose to its feet again then growled at Dyphestive, walked over to him, and knocked him over. It roared in his face with hot, fetid breath.

Dyphestive slugged the gourn in the lower jaw, and its legs wobbled, and it fell.

One of the Doom Riders gasped. Dyphestive wasn't sure which one it was, but they were as shocked as he was.

Scar rushed over to his gourn with a stunned look on his face. He knelt down beside it and said, "Get up, beast. Get up."

Dyphestive looked at his right hand and opened and closed his fingers. At first, he thought that they might have been broken, but they only stung. He'd hit the gourn hard, but he didn't think he'd hit it that hard, either. *How'd I do that?*

The gourn rolled its neck and shook its head.

Dyphestive noticed the water skin lying on the dusty ground nearby. He crawled over to it and picked it up.

"Don't you dare, boy," Scar said.

"Let him drink," Drysis said. "He earned it."

Dyphestive gulped down the water then showered his face with the rest and squeezed it until none was left. He tossed the water skin at Scar's feet. "You're empty."

33

Rhonna was standing over a stone marker and a grave recently covered with stones. She and Lythlenion were at a cemetery half a league from Raven Cliff. It was early evening, and Zora and Tanlin were with them, carrying lanterns.

"That's Browning's grave," Zora said. She held a handkerchief to her nose and sniffed. "We never knew much about him. No family or anything. A lifelong soldier."

Rhonna nodded. For some reason, Zora had opened up to her at Tanlin's Fine Fittings. It seemed that Zora knew who she was the moment she saw her. Apparently, Grey Cloak and Dyphestive had mentioned her in detail. "Sorry to hear about your friends. All of them."

Zora and Tanlin had shared all that they'd been through with Grey Cloak and Dyphestive. The charming pair of rogues were clearly shaken by the sudden loss of their friends.

Beside Browning's grave was a headstone with the words Grey Cloak chiseled on it.

"We didn't know what to do about Grey Cloak," Zora said as she kneeled and dusted the marker off with her hand. "We never found a body in Lovers' Gorge. Only some blood and strips of clothing." Her chin quivered, but she fought off the crying. "It appeared that some sort of wild beasts took him."

"No body?" Lythlenion asked curiously.

"That's why we didn't dig a grave, like Browning's," Zora said. "We only covered the spot in stones to honor him." She patted the headstone. "He was sweet. Cocky but sweet. I wish I'd had that dinner with him."

"Where are the other graves?" Lythlenion asked. "Dalsay and Adanadel? Is that correct?"

Zora stood up and wiped her eyes. She tried to speak but suddenly couldn't talk.

Tanlin set his lantern down and rubbed Zora's shoulders. "We've risked our lives together on Dalsay's quests. Any one of us could have died, and some had, but this incident was different. It felt like we witnessed a cold and calculating murder." He sighed. "As for Dalsay, well, Tatiana took him to the Wizard Watch. Mages such as he have unique customs. And we saw to it that Adanadel was returned to Monarch City for a proper burial. He was a knight of the monarch, and he had family."

Zora buried her face in Tanlin's chest.

Tanlin went on. "The strange thing was that Grey Cloak told us that they had an encounter with a Sky Rider named Anya. When we found that out, we sent word to Dalsay, because he always emphasized that no incident should be taken as a coincidence. Every encounter has a meaning. He came back to Raven Cliff immediately to seek out Grey Cloak and Dyphestive. He said that they were *naturals*."

"Sounds like you had a pair of unique farmhands working for you," Lythlenion said to Rhonna.

"I wish they were still working on the farm now." Rhonna was familiar with naturals. They were unique people who in many cases became dragon riders. Something else was still eating at her mind, however. "Zora, I don't mean to doubt you, but do you have more than Grey Cloak's garment?"

"The only other thing I had was his boot. It was in the street. I sold it to him when we met in the shop." Zora pointed at the grave. "I buried it in there." New tears began to flow down her face. "I feel horrible about all of it. They were young, and I took advantage of them."

"That's what thieves do," Rhonna said bluntly. "It catches up with you, but you and Tanlin seem all right for a pair of rogues. Would you take me to the spot where Grey Cloak died? I would like to see it for myself."

"Certainly," Zora said.

After a long walk, they entered the gorge inside the cliff face. The gorge was only thirty yards wide at the entrance, and it really wasn't a gorge by normal standards. It was more of an oversized crevice in the cliff face, a natural gap that nature had hewn out of the cliffs. It was five hundred feet to the top and narrowed to only ten to fifteen yards across inside.

"I believe he tried to jump the gap," Tanlin said as he pointed upward. "And landed somewhere in this area. This is where we found the torn shirt."

"Do you mind?" Rhonna took Tanlin's lantern. The gorge was dark day or night, but the lantern's glow helped. There were small cave openings in the rocks and paw prints on the ground in some spots. "What lives in these caves?" she asked as she peered inside of one.

Tanlin and Zora shrugged.

"Judging by these paw prints, I think they might be wolverines or badgers. The prints are very big. A small bear, maybe," Tanlin said.

"Did Grey Cloak carry anything else?" Rhonna asked.

"He had a sword belt," Zora said as she picked her lip. "I checked his room at the inn. Nothing was there, aside from Dyphestive's iron sword and his anvil."

"Anvil?" Rhonna asked. "A small one?"

"Maybe thirty pounds," Zora replied.

"And here I thought that I misplaced it. Why in Gapoli

would he take that? Huh." She scanned the ground. A silver chip was sticking out of the dirt inside one of the cave entrances. "Maybe this was his."

"That would be a long shot," Tanlin said. "Many people cast coins off of the bridge and make wishes. But thieves and scavengers from the villages take them. Many times, they fight over them."

Rhonna pocketed the coin. "There wasn't anything else in their room?"

"I think everything that Grey Cloak owned, he kept on himself. He didn't seem like the kind to leave it."

"Sounds about right. Still..." Rhonna squatted in front of the cave. The openings were big enough for a person to crawl into or be dragged inside. It was impossible to guess how deep it went without going in. Rhonna got on her hands and knees and crawled inside.

"Rhonna, what are you doing?" Lythlenion asked desperately.

"I'm looking for a body!" She'd already made it ten feet in and dragged the lantern with her.

Lythlenion hollered into the tunnel, "Don't be surprised if you find a furry body with fangs bigger than your fingers."

"I won't be."

"SORRY," Lythlenion said to Zora and Tanlin, "but she can be impulsive at times."

"It's quite all right. Dwarfs have grit. It's no surprise," Tanlin said.

"So you didn't know Grey Cloak or Dyphestive?" Zora asked.

"No, I'm afraid not. I wish I had. Perhaps I will. One thing is for certain," Lythlenion said as he studied the cave entrance. "Rhonna cared deeply for them, and she doesn't care about anything."

34

That night, Rhonna rented the room that Grey Cloak and Dyphestive had been staying in. She worked on the broken shutters in exchange for a break in the fee. She couldn't help working on things, and she always brought some small tools everywhere she went.

"Your vision was right. My friends were in danger, but it was too late," she said to Lythlenion, who was lying on Dyphestive's bed with his hands behind his head.

"They aren't always right, which is why I don't like to use that spell. But usually, it tells you enough to be helpful." He closed his eyes. "What do you want to do now?"

Since Rhonna had been in the room, she'd replayed the battle that took place in her head. A floorboard was cracked, and the top of a bedpost had been knocked off. The hinges on the door were loose.

According to a patron she'd questioned, two Doom Riders, one in a red mask and the other in a green one, had entered and thrown Dyphestive out of the window.

"I don't know. I can't shake the feeling that Grey Cloak is still here." She'd scoured the caves in the gorge the best she could but found no sign of Grey Cloak anywhere. They'd even talked to local villagers in the valley below the city. Now one saw anything. "Do you think that you could use that spell to see if he is alive?"

Lythlenion opened an eye. "I'm going to need something. An object. The same as the last time." He rolled onto his side and looked underneath the bed then dragged the iron sword across the floor. "I could use this."

"Well, I'm pretty sure that Dyphestive is alive, and we know where he is heading." She picked up the small anvil that Dyphestive had carried and tossed it up and down. It was so strange that out of all of the objects he could have taken from her smithy, he'd chosen that one. "That's another problem, but first things first."

"We don't have much to use, do we."

"Not on us, but that grave that Zora made for Grey Cloak does."

"You want to go back there?"

"Do you think your spell will work?"

"It will work, but that doesn't mean that you'll find out what you want." He stuck the two-handed sword point first in the floor and ran his fingers down the metal. "This is made for a big man. How big is Dyphestive?"

"Bigger than you and as strong as an ox."

"I see. Do we want to tell Zora and Tanlin what we are planning?"

"Of course not. They are thieves, and even though they are amiable, I'm not the type of person who takes a shine to those who thrive dishonestly."

"Understood." He stood up. "Shall we go?"

Without lanterns, they made their way through the night and covered the distance to the cemetery in less than an hour. The cemetery was acres of rolling hills rich in ancient willow trees. The gentle breeze over the plains stirred the soft greenery of the willow leaves, giving them the appearance of living things.

Rhonna found Grey Cloak's and Browning's graves. She bent over and grabbed a rock on Grey Cloak's plot.

"Wait," Lythlenion said.

She eyed him. "You aren't getting superstitious on me, are you? Grey Cloak isn't buried here."

"I know, but I really don't want to risk disturbing any other restless spirits that might wander the fields." He removed a small tobacco pouch from inside of his clothing then took a pinch of something green and sprinkled it over the stones. "Rasbine. A special herb from my gardens that the spooks don't like." He sprinkled more on Browning's as well. "That should do it."

Rhonna began removing the stones one by one. Buried underneath a shallow pile of stones was a leather sack. She opened up the sack and dumped the boot out. The crushed leather was soft in her hand. For some reason, her throat tightened, and she wiped an eye. "He hated shoes. I think he thought that he would have to work if he wore them." She handed it to Lythlenion.

"We can't do it here. We are going to need a campfire."

"That slipped my mind." She looked about. "I suppose we can build one not so far from here." She pointed to the wood line beyond the field of graves. "Let's get moving."

They made a fire inside the cover of the forest, away from any prying eyes. The orange flames devoured the dry wood they had gathered.

Lythlenion scattered some pine needles over the flames, turning them black. He held the boot in his rough-looking hands. "No guarantees."

"Do it."

He dropped the boot on the flames. Before long, the leather started to smoke and stink. He took more mystic herbs from one of his pouches and spread them over the flames. The fire turned bright pink and purple. A figurine of flame held the boot up, and Lythlenion began chanting softly.

The boot burst into flames. A ring of multicolored fire the size of a plate formed around it. The boot leather dried up into ashes, and the night wind took it away. Only blackness appeared inside the ring—stark, empty, lonely darkness, a void that the firelight did not fill. Then the ring of fire shrank and diminished, and only the campfire flames were left.

"I'm sorry, Rhonna," Lythlenion said. "I can't say for certain, but I think that means that Grey Cloak is dead."

She shook her head and mumbled, "I don't believe it. Perhaps there was another meaning."

"I've used that spell many times and have never seen an empty image. I wish that the outcome could have been better. Again, I'm sorry."

Rhonna hung her head and turned her back to the flames. "It's not your fault. It's mine."

35

Across the street from the inn where Rhonna and Lythlenion were staying, Grey Cloak watched their room window from the alley's shadows. He was crouched down, with his cloak draped around his body and the hood pulled over his head. *What to do? What to do? What to do?*

A trio of drunk men filed into the alley. The cheerful men walked right past him, stood against the buildings, and relieved themselves while singing. *Ew!*

One of the men looked in Grey Cloak's direction and grunted. "Do you see what I see? I think that's a person."

"Come on," one of the other men said. "You're seeing things. Probably two of everything."

"I see three," the third man said. He threw his arms over the shoulders of the other two men and led them out of the alley. "Yo doddley dee, a pirate's life for we?"

"*Hiccup.* We aren't pirates. We sell china."

"Aye, but tonight, we tell the girls—*buuurp*—we are pirates."

"But we aren't dressed like pirates," the second man replied. He had a higher-pitched voice than the others.

"All you have to do is tell them that this is how—*hiccup*—pirates dress on shore leave."

"I think it would make more sense if we said we were sailors."

Their voices faded as they ventured farther away in the streets.

Grey Cloak moved out of the alley and huddled in front of the porch beside the trough. He kept his eyes on the room window while hiding the best he could from passersby. Though it was late at night, there was plenty of activity as men and women moved from tavern to tavern. It wasn't anything like the night that Grey Cloak had been trapped by the Doom Riders. The streets had been barren, as a curfew had been imposed. The thought that the Doom Riders were aided by the leaders of Raven Cliff angered him, but he had more important issues to deal with. *I can't believe that Rhonna is here.*

Rhonna was the last person that he'd ever expected to see again. Yet there she was, searching for him. He'd come across her when he was spying on Zora and Tanlin. After he was chased into Lovers' Gorge by the Doom Riders, he'd replayed everything that happened in his mind. He couldn't stop thinking about it. And until he was ready, he wasn't going to let anyone know that he was alive, because he feared that Tanlin and Zora might have been in on his and Dyphestive's demise.

A beggar in tattered clothing teetered out of the alley. He was an older man, and he moved toward Grey Cloak and tried to nestle in the same spot by the porch and water trough. He let out a startled "Gah!" when he bumped into Grey Cloak.

"Go away, beggar," Grey Cloak commanded. "I was here first."

"This is my spot for beggin'. Always my spot!" The beggar bowed his back and clawed the air with his fingers. "You go away."

Grey Cloak pulled his dagger and passed it by the man's eyes. "My spot."

The beggar made a nimble jump backward and said, "Never threaten a beggar. A beggar knows more than you." He made a bizarre cackle and hustled away.

Beggars. He slid his dagger back in his scabbard then looked up at the inn window and noticed Rhonna sitting on the sill. Her head was turned right toward him. *She must have seen the dustup. Thanks a lot, beggar.*

He held his position until a horse-drawn wagon passed by. Then he slipped back into the alley and climbed the wall adjacent to the building. He crept across the roof and ducked into the moon's shadow cast over a chimney. From that spot, he could still see Rhonna. Her stocky body was leaning out of the window. *She couldn't have known that was me, could she?*

Rhonna leaned back inside the room and pulled the window closed.

Good. He waited, watched, and contemplated. Once again, he recollected everything that had happened at Lovers' Gorge.

The Doom Riders had chased him down the street. With all avenues of escape cut off, except for the cliffs, he opted to jump the gorge. Running at full speed, he made the leap for the railing. He made it over halfway and quickly found himself clawing at the air, grasping for anything. As the rocky gorge promised to swallow him in its jagged teeth, he could only think of one thing.

Stop falling!

With less than fifty feet left before fatal impact, the folds of his cloak billowed to life. The air was trapped under his cloak and broke his rapid descent. He hit the ground like a bird with a broken wing crashing, but it was more than enough to save him. The jarring impact knocked the breath out of him, but he was alive.

His first inclination was to get up and run, but another thought struck him. He lay on the ground and played dead. In his black grave in the gorge, he didn't move, and with his heart thumping in his ears, he listened with his keen hearing.

Drysis and the Doom Riders talked about whether or not to climb down and check on him, but they opted to wait and watch. It was the longest hour of Grey Cloak's life as he strained to hear any scuffle or murmuring that they made. He picked up the sound of soft voices, heavy breathing, and the rustling of the gourns' saddles and bridles. He envisioned all four of them and where they were stationed.

Finally, they moved away. Grey Cloak continued to lie still for a long time, until a scuffle came out of the caves. He twisted around and came face-to-face with a man-sized wolverine. He socked it in the nose and half limped, half sprinted out of the gorge. He'd been hiding ever since, ashamed, while every waking moment, he thought about his blood brother, Dyphestive. *I have to save him, but I can't do it alone. Who can I trust?*

36

After surviving the fall at Lovers' Gorge, Grey Cloak had lain low. He'd dirtied his clothing and kept to the streets of Raven Cliff. He was still barefoot too. The first thing he wanted to do was free Dyphestive, but he knew that he didn't stand a chance against the Doom Riders. Instead, he sought out Talon. By spying on Zora and Tanlin, he saw Adanadel being sent home and Tatiana leaving with Dalsay's body. From a distance, he watched Browning get buried.

Disguised as one of the groundskeepers, he had to choke down the tears at Browning's funeral. It was only Tanlin and Zora. He overheard Tanlin's kind words about a jovial, big-hearted but otherwise lonely man who gave his all to save Grey Cloak and Dyphestive.

Grey Cloak had stuck to Tanlin and Zora after that. As

much as he liked them both, they'd deceived him before, and they were the only ones from the battle with the Doom Riders to be unscathed.

Being raised in Dark Mountain, Grey Cloak had learned that very few people could be trusted. He'd seen good people with the best intentions turned inside out and become workers of evil. Friends, older ones, had succumbed to the dark vices the older they became and the more training they were exposed to. He'd known he had to get out, that he and Dyphestive had to escape or become something else.

As for Zora, he liked her very much... perhaps too much. Using the cover of other people, carts, yurts, and wagons, he spied on her. He saw her talking to people that he'd never met and watched folks with the appearance of power and persuasion enter Tanlin's store. He was certain they were up to something, until he saw her crying when she delivered flowers to the spot where Dalsay, Adanadel, and Browning had fallen.

His heart swelled. He knew her tears were real. Grey Cloak decided to reveal himself, when the unexpected intervened. He waited for Zora to return to the store from across the street and saw Rhonna enter Tanlin's Fittings. Rhonna wasn't alone, either. She was with an orc, a real bruiser with blond hair and a war mace made for a killer. At that point, more conspiracies started to swirl in his head.

Is Rhonna an agent of evil? Does she serve Black Frost? How does she know Zora and Tanlin?

After shadowing them to Browning's grave, he quickly learned the truth. Rhonna had come to protect him and Dyphestive, but she and her friend Lythlenion were too late. Then the question was if he should reveal himself to Rhonna or if they would all be better off if they thought he was dead. *What would Dyphestive do?*

Rhonna might not have been the most pleasant person, but she was straightforward. She worked their fingers to the bone and never let up. She'd hardened both of them but in a good way and saw to it that they had just what they needed and nothing more. The problem was, she scared Grey Cloak, and he'd stolen from her, sort of.

I'll do it. He looked at the great dragon constellations in the sky. *I'll do it for Dyphestive because he needs my help.*

He edged out of the chimney's shadow and low-walked to the edge of the building where the roof overlooked the alley. It was clear, so he spread the folds of his cloak and jumped. He dropped quickly at first then slowed and landed as softly as a feather. Grinning, he thought, *I don't know what this cloak is, but it's amazing.*

Since he'd accidently discovered the cloak's power during his fall at Lovers' Gorge, he'd been tinkering with it. The cloak had become a second skin to him. When he first had it, it didn't have any pockets, but after he thought about it, it had pockets. He could place a coin in one pocket and pluck it out of another as he wanted.

The same power worked with the falling. He'd jumped off of several buildings. The cloak wouldn't slow his fall until he thought about it, then he would float down like a leaf. If the cloak had other powers, he hadn't discovered them yet.

He started across the street. *Here I go.*

Grey Cloak didn't make it two steps before he caught Tanlin and Zora coming down the street. He moved back into the alley. Zora had an angry look on her face. Her fists were balled up at her sides, and the belt of daggers dressing her hips had a nice sway to them. *She's even prettier when she's angry.*

Tanlin hooked her arm just before Zora entered the inn. "Let me handle this," he said.

"No," she replied and stormed inside.

Tanlin vanished inside with her.

Grey Cloak made his move. He dashed across the street and hopped silently onto the covered porch. His strong fingers latched onto the wood siding of the inn, and using his toes, he quickly crawled up the wall. Once he made it to the top, he hovered over Rhonna's window. He arrived in time, just as hard knocking started on the door inside.

"Who is it?" Rhonna asked gruffly.

The floorboards in the room groaned. Grey Cloak

heard a blade sliding out of a sheath. He leaned farther over the ledge.

"It's Zora and Tanlin!" Zora said. "We demand a word with you!"

The hinges on the door squeaked.

"By all means, come in," Rhonna said.

"It's lovely to see you again," Lythlenion added.

"Stuff your pleasantries, you grave robbers. I know what you did," Zora said. "You tried to dig up Grey Cloak and Browning."

"We did no such thing," Rhonna fired back. "And you'd better kettle that tone, girl. I don't care for that sort of talk."

With the streets clear at the moment, Grey Cloak lowered himself down from the roof and hung from one hand and planted his toes on the windowsill. He could see though the gaps in the shutters. Zora's cheeks were as red as roses. Tanlin was standing behind her with a worried expression.

"Really?" Zora glowered down at Rhonna. "And what are you going to do? Turn me over your knee and whip me?"

"I've whipped bigger than you, you little sass!" Rhonna said.

"Ladies, please, we can sort this out," Lythlenion said as he wedged himself between them. "It's all a misunderstanding."

"No, it isn't," Zora said. "You stole from a grave. Admit it!"

"Mind your business, thief!" Rhonna said.

"You sound like the pot calling the kettle black. Mind your own business, dwarf!"

"This *is* my business!"

Grey Cloak put his full weight on the windowsill. *All of this fighting over me. I like it. And I've never seen Rhonna so worked up before. I didn't know she had it in her.*

"Oy! What are you doing up there, you peeker?" a man shouted from the street. "Get down from there!" The rotund man cupped his hands around his mouth and shouted, "Thief! Thief! Thief!"

37

Grey Cloak started to shush the man but thought the better of it. He quietly said to the man in the street, "I'm not stealing. I merely misplaced my key."

"Thief! Thief! Thief! Someone fetch the patrol!"

This isn't working. And where did that man come from? The streets were clear a moment ago. He decided to climb back onto the roof.

Rhonna flung the shutters open. She saw him hanging in the window and gasped.

"Hello, Rhonna," he said with a sheepish grin. "How have you been?"

"How have I *been*? *Where* have you been?" Rhonna yelled. She grabbed him by the cloak and jerked him inside then locked her arms around his waist and squeezed him in a bear hug, lifting him off the floor.

"Grey Cloak!" Zora said, her eyes filled with shock.

"Hello, Zora." He grimaced. "Nice to see you again."

Rhonna set him down.

The moment his toes touched the floor, Zora rushed him. She tackled him on the bed and peppered his face with kisses. *I knew she liked me.*

Zora pinned him down and with her brow knitted, she asked, "*Where have you been?*" She let him sit up.

"Um... hiding."

"Well, you did a fine job of it. We've been searching for you everywhere," Zora said. "But I thought for certain that you were dead." She teared up, but her face turned angry. "I should kill you for making me feel this way."

"I'm sorry, but after everything that happened..." He paused, not wanting to tell her that he didn't trust her. So he kept that to himself. He told a half-truth... or half-lie, not that there was much of a difference. "I was scared."

"You aren't the only one," Tanlin said. He gave Grey Cloak a hug. "We all were. I still am."

He caught Lythlenion looking at him. The blond orc appeared as rough as any orc, but his features were soft and warm, making him less intimidating than the man he'd seen from a distance. "Hello."

Lythlenion extended his hand. "I'm Lythlenion. It's very nice to meet you, and I'm glad to discover that you are alive. Rhonna was the only one who believed you still were. Perhaps it was a mother's intuition."

"I'm not his mother," Rhonna said with her arms crossed. "He's an elf. I'm a dwarf. Impossible."

Grey Cloak stood, approached Rhonna, and said, "The truth is, you are the only mother I've ever known."

"Ah, that's nice," Zora said.

"Why did you come for me?" he asked.

Rhonna told him about the Doom Riders' arrival in Havenstock.

He sat down and took it all in. Burying his face in his hands, he sighed. "They killed Griff. The old half ogre didn't do anything."

"Drysis wanted to make a point," Rhonna said. "She made it clear that if I got involved, I would die. Heh. Like I'm going to listen to that white-haired witch."

A lot of mixed emotions began to swell up inside Grey Cloak. He had a hard time catching his breath. "This is all my fault. All of it. No one would have died if I'd remained at Dark Mountain."

Zora took her place beside him and put her hand around his waist. "No one blames you. And you can't blame yourself. You only did what you had to do to survive."

"How can you say that? Griff, Dalsay, Adanadel, and Browning are all dead because of me. And Dyphestive is going right back to where he started. Of course it's my fault. I wanted this, and look what happened."

"Don't start feeling sorry for yourself now," Rhonna

said in her firm voice. "That won't bring back the dead. What matters is, what are you going to do now?"

"And Drysis thinks you are dead," Tanlin pointed out. "That's a new start for you."

"New start?" He gave a fragile laugh. "I'm not going to abandon Dyphestive. I'm going after him, but I need help." A quiet fell over the room as Grey Cloak searched their faces.

Tanlin broke the silence. "I don't mean to sound like a coward, but even Dalsay, Adanadel, and Browning, the strongest members of Talon, couldn't slow the Doom Riders. Without them, how can we even stand a chance? They are killers. I'm very sorry, but Zora and I will have to stay out of it."

"Speak for yourself," Zora said. "I will help you any way that I can. You're going to need the mind of a good thief if you are going to steal somebody."

"Thanks," he said, "but I don't want you getting hurt too. You would be safer in Raven Cliff. This is your home."

"I have no home. I've been a roamer since birth," she said.

"I didn't come all this way to fetch the one of you," Rhonna said. "I came to get you both back. I believe I speak for both of us when I say that Lythlenion and I are in."

Lythlenion nodded. "I've always wanted to see Dark Mountain this time of year."

Grey Cloak managed a smirk. He remembered what the

old hermit had told him. "Steal a Dragon. Save the world." The only thing he was going to steal was his brother. He stood and looked at Tanlin. "Can we still call ourselves Talon?"

"I don't see why not. We are the only ones who are left."

"I guess it's us against the world," Grey Cloak said as he raised his middle and index fingers and thumb. He made a claw with them.

Zora, Rhonna, and Lythlenion made a circle and made the same gesture. They all cast a look Tanlin's way.

"Oh, all right." Tanlin joined the circle and raised his hand. "Who wants to live forever, anyway? Or even another week."

Grey Cloak nodded. "It's time to shred our enemies and get my brother back. Long live Talon."

38

DARK MOUNTAIN

Dread. Dyphestive had known the feeling before, but it was worse than ever. His young life had come full circle, and once again, he was working in the bowels of Dark Mountain under heavy guard.

With his arms and legs shackled with heavy chains, he pushed a large wooden cart down a wide cave tunnel lit by torchlight. He was in the Dragon Hive, a network of caves where the Riskers' dragons slept. The aisles were paved with stone, and the dragons' stables had been hewn right out of the natural rock. Most of the stables were twice as big as horse stables, and others were ten to twenty times the size of those.

In front of each stable was a steel gate that lowered like a portcullis and sealed the dragons inside. There were over a hundred of the assorted stables, on both sides of the aisle, which stretched on for two hundred yards.

The wheels on the cart that Dyphestive was pushing creaked. His chains rattled and scraped over the ground when he walked. He lifted a shovel with a wide head out of the cart and leaned it over his shoulder.

There were two soldiers standing nearby. They were wearing chain mail underneath black tunics. Open-faced bronze helmets with a black plume of steel feathers on the top covered their heads. Their tunics had bronze dragon faces on the chest. Bullwhips and longswords hung from their belts. They never spoke.

Ten of the stables' steel gates were pulled up. Dyphestive took his shovel into the nearest one. He hadn't even been back in Dark Mountain half a day, and he was already doing what he'd dreaded as a boy—cleaning the dragon stables. But it was different. He was guarded and didn't have the liberties he'd had before. He was without his brother too.

His nose crinkled. The dung caught fire like wood and stank even worse. "Uck. Dragon dung. The smell you never get used to." He held his breath and started shoveling out the dung. He carried a shovelful out of the stable and dumped it in then went back and forth two more times. The dragons were relatively clean creatures, not much different from horses, but their poops were heavier. He finished cleaning out that stable and went to the next. After he cleaned all ten of them out, he took the wagon back down the tunnel.

At the front end of the tunnel was a series of larger man-made barn chambers where more stone had been carved into caves. A ring of cut obsidian encompassed the volcanic fires of the mountain. He parked the cart beside it and began shoveling the dragon dung in.

After Dyphestive finished the job, he reloaded the cart with straw and pulled it back down the tunnel and covered the floors of the dragon stables with the new straw. Then he looked at the soldiers and asked, "When do I eat?"

The soldiers didn't reply. Instead, the taller one of the two pointed down the tunnel.

"I guess I can eat straw if I have to." He started pulling the cart. The farther he went, the larger the stable doors became. All of them were closed. He couldn't say for sure, but he thought each and every one of them had a dragon inside. The ones that he'd cleaned being empty meant that the dragons had been moved or were doing drills with the Riskers. The dragons and their riders did a lot of training. He and Grey Cloak had avoided them for good reason.

To his right, near the end of the tunnel, the gate of a huge stable was open. His heart skipped as he approached. It was Bonfire's stable. She was the dragon that had aided his and Grey Cloak's escape from Dark Mountain. He'd been so busy thinking about himself and his rumbling tummy that he'd forgotten all about her. *She's still here!*

He pushed the cart faster. He wasn't alone. He had a friend. Bonfire was an ancient dragon, so old that she slept so much that they left her stable open. For years, she never moved, but one day, the dragon's eyes had opened, and she spoke. Bonfire told them how to escape... how to have hope.

With his chains rattling around his ankles, and the shovel over his shoulder, he hustled to Bonfire's stable. Her elephant-sized form was huddled in the darkness, and he crept farther in. "Bonfire," he said quietly. "It's me."

The closer he got, the more he saw. Yards deep and against the wall was the shape of a dragon. "No," he said as he rushed inside. Scorch marks of dragon fire were all over the stone inside the stable. The strong scent of sulfur lingered in the air. He stood in front of Bonfire's skull. Nothing was left of her but scales and bones. He sank to his knees and lay on the bridge of her nose and sobbed. "No."

39

"Are you glad to be back home?" Drysis asked Dyphestive. She was leading him, shackles and all, to the main tower of Dark Mountain.

"This isn't my home," he said. His foot got tangled in his chains, and he shook it loose. He'd been breaking his back for hours, cleaning more stables, when she arrived.

"Of course this is your home. You were born here." Drysis walked with her broad shoulders back and her chin high. She carried herself more like a queen than a warrior. "All of us were born here."

"Things don't come here to be born. They come to die," he said.

"My, aren't you morbid. And deep. Surprising for one so young." She led him out of the caves to the surface of Dark Mountain. The tapestry of rocky hills and steep inclines was surrounded by small volcanos bubbling with lava. A broad roadway snaked at least a league up toward the mountain peak to the castle-like citadel nestled at the top.

The sky was dreary and cloudy. Lightning flashed, but no rain came. The strong winds whistled through the jagged rocks on the stark and endless hills that stretched on as far as the eye could see.

Dyphestive craned his neck. The dim skies weren't empty. Dragons were jetting through the expanse, soaring in all directions with wings wide. The winged monsters' bodies had hard ridges and dark scales outlined with colors glinting between their spiny ridges. Their scales had colorful splashes like turtle skin, shining like gemstones and diamonds. They had emerald, sapphire, sunburst yellow, pink, silver, copper, and obsidian. No one dragon's colors were the same. They were all unique in one way or the other, with their underlying colors on their faces like masks.

"If I were you, I would be glad to return here. Who knows? One day, you could be one of them," Drysis said as she watched the dragons flying above. "Being a Risker is the highest honor."

"I thought being a Sky Rider was."

"All of the Sky Riders are dead," she answered.

He knew better. He'd seen Anya. *I hope she wasn't the last one.*

A dragon and its rider buzzed over them, and Dyphestive got a glimpse of the young man in the saddle. His name was Dirklen, and he'd been brought up with Dyphestive but was a little older. Now, he was wearing the full armor and dragon face helmet of a Risker.

Dirklen made another pass. His intense eyes locked on Dyphestive's. He spit, tugged on his dragon's reins, and veered toward the top of the mountain.

"Did you know him?" Drysis asked. "I don't think he likes you. Of course, most won't since you abandoned them. You would probably be better off if you were dead. Or you'll wish you were soon enough."

He eyed her and asked, "Where are we going?"

"To the top."

He gave her a puzzled look and asked, "Why?"

"Because Black Frost summoned you. That's why."

Dyphestive's heavy chains became heavier, his heart dropped into his toes, and his pace slowed. *Why me? Oh no, why me?*

Drysis grabbed the chain between his wrist cuffs and tugged him along like a child. "There is a price that you must pay when you leave here. Consequences. I don't know what that price will be, but I wouldn't want to be in your boots. The penalty for desertion and disloyalty is very stiff. Often fatal. I'm surprised that he still wants you alive."

Me too.

Drysis angled toward the side of the roadway, stopped, and looked over the wall. It was quite a drop into the black teeth of the canyon. "Many have been summoned to Black Frost's throne only to never return. Some of them jumped off of this very road rather than face him. Which would you rather do?"

Dyphestive looked her in the eye and said, "I would rather face the dragon that sent you to kill my friends."

"You are angry. Good, you'll need that. But in the presence of Black Frost, it won't last. Fear will consume you. Your will to live will die. If you live, you'll be reborn. And if you die, well, you'll be dead just like countless others."

They made it to the base of the rectangular citadel that capped the mountain peak. It had no doors or windows, and dragons that were perched like gargoyles replaced battlements at the top. Icicles hung from the edges. Its black rock surface was smooth all over. It measured over one hundred yards from side to side. It was another hundred yards from the bottom to the top, with an outer stairwell.

"This way," she said.

The stairs' breadth was barely big enough for one person. There was no railing. The staircase went outside and inside on the way up the citadel. Dyphestive's toes dangled from the edge from time to time.

"Careful. One slip, and you'll fall to your doom," Drysis said as she navigated the steps with the surefooted ease of a cat. Even with the wind throwing her white hair across her face and half covering her eyes, she moved like she'd walked the steps a thousand times before. "Almost there."

Dyphestive lumbered along behind her watching her every step. She was the woman who had killed his friends, and she was being coy with him. *I hope you fall.*

Only one flight of steps was left between them and the top. Dyphestive's heart began to race.

Drysis paused and took a quick breath then gave Dyphestive a final glance and said, "Your moment of truth has come."

40

Dyphestive stood beside Drysis on the flat top of the citadel as the chill winds tore through his hair. At first, he didn't notice anything on the icy platform. He'd seen plenty of dragons, small and large, the biggest being Cinder, whom he'd met with Anya. Having never seen Black Frost before, Dyphestive had thought he would be a dragon like Cinder, possibly bigger.

But he was wrong. Very wrong.

Dyphestive's fingers went numb as he followed Drysis's stare. His mouth hung open as his eyes swept over the astounding length of the abominable beast. *Black Frost! Impossible!*

Lying on the expansive platform was a dragon stretched out from one end to the other. He was ten times bigger than any dragon Dyphestive had ever imagined. His hulking body stretched thirty yards long. The wings folded behind his back were like great ship sails that were as black as night. Layers of black and deep-blue scales covered his gargantuan body with the size and thickness of a knight's shield. The talons on his feet were as long as a man's height. Mounds of hard, spiny ridges covered his body. The winged juggernaut was to a dragon what a sparrow was to a man.

Drysis set her eyes on Dyphestive. "Don't forget to breathe."

He caught his breath and nodded.

The spiked tip of Black Frost's tail twitched, and his scales rippled from the tip of his tail to the end of his body. The appendage ran half the length of his body. *Come!*

The word shook Dyphestive to the bone. He didn't know if he'd heard it or if it was in his head. He couldn't see the dragon's face because his neck was bent toward the other side.

Even Drysis's face paled as she towed Dyphestive down the platform. They angled around the dragon's body like a bend in a hillside. Black Frost stared right at them with huge yellow eyes that burned like the sun. His humongous head was as black as coal, and blue scales made a frightening mask. His horns curled like a ram's and pointed straight back. Giant fangs jutted from the sides of his mouth. His breath was so cold that it was suffocating.

Drysis kneeled and pulled Dyphestive down with her. "I have done as you commanded, my king," she said.

"Have you, now?" Black Frost asked in a voice that resonated like thunder. "I only see one traitor, not two."

Black Frost's mammoth jaws were as big as the tunnels in the stables. Dyphestive felt like a bird that had landed on a horse's back by comparison. He never would have believed something living could be so large.

"The other traitor died," Drysis said with her head still bowed.

"You killed him?" Black Frost asked, impatience clear in his voice.

"No. He died in the pursuit. He fell through a chasm, and it crushed him."

"I see." Black Frost clacked his teeth together. "I ordered you to bring them back, both alive, did I not?"

"Yes, my king," she said.

"Hence, you failed, yet you deny it."

"My king, I-I..." Her voice started to tremble, and her head dipped farther. "I failed."

"Yes, you did." Black Frost growled. "I'm not sure which I hate more, failure or excuses." His giant talons *click-clacked* on the icy deck. "Today, it is excuses. You were wise not to give me one. Next time will be the last one." He dragged his head around and faced Dyphestive. His nostrils flared as he sniffed. "Ah... a young natural. Why did you betray me, child?"

Dyphestive couldn't say or think of anything. His insides and outsides were frozen stiff.

Black Frost eyed him up and down then lifted a foot and held it over Dyphestive's head. "Young and big. Unique." He sniffed again. "I smell great strength in this one. Hmm..."

Dyphestive's tongue loosed. "I wanted to be free to live for myself."

Black Frost's head tilted from side to side like a ship at sea slowly pitching against the waves. "Interesting. I don't take you for one to think independently. It was the other one, wasn't it, that plotted your escape."

"I helped."

The dragon gave a frosty laugh. "You are a terrible liar." He touched Dyphestive on the noggin with the tip of his black claw. "And not very smart, either. I don't think you are suited to be a Risker. Not after three years. You're beyond the ripening age. The question is, do I spare you or eat you?" He pushed his enormous head off the ground and rose to a sitting position.

Dyphestive leaned his head backward. Black Frost was several stories tall. The gray scales on his stomach and chest were bigger than he was. He searched for a weakness on Black Frost's spectacular body, but the seams between his scales were tight, and his powerful muscles bulged underneath his scaly skin. He had no weakness that could be seen. *How can anyone stop such a monster?*

"How do our other missions in the field fare?" Black Frost asked Drysis.

"Several agents in the field are gathering dragon charms. A group called the Scourge has pledged their loyalty to you, my king. They have had great success thwarting the allies of the Wizard Watch."

"Good. See to it that they resume their quest." Black Frost cast a glance into the skies. "I have decided." His penetrating gaze landed on Drysis. "You will take this youth and turn him into a Doom Rider. If he resists the training, kill him."

41

DAGGERFORD

The new members of Talon rode into Daggerford on horseback in the wee hours of the night. The town didn't have much—it was a last-stop border town between Ugrad and Westerlund. The citizens weren't known for farming or mining or much of anything at all. It was the sort of place a person could get lost and never be found again. At least, that was the feeling that Grey Cloak got as they passed the dreary buildings. He liked it. *I wish I'd come here first. I might have saved Dyphestive and myself a heap of trouble.*

"What do you think?" Zora asked Rhonna. Bleary eyed, she scanned the buildings. "I need sleep."

"Sleep. Hah," Rhonna said. "I can sleep where I'm sitting if I need to. But I know that elves require a good measure of beauty sleep to keep up appearances."

"I sleep a lot, and it hasn't done a thing for me," Lythlenion commented.

Zora shot daggers at Rhonna. They'd bickered the entire trip. "I don't have a problem sleeping on the ground from time to time. I've slept on floors for most of my life, but if I can have a soft bed and a pillow, then I'll gladly take it."

"Suit yourself. There are plenty of places for you to lay your pretty little head," Rhonna scoffed.

Zora pulled her horse away and rode back to Grey Cloak. "And you lived with her for three years. You're a better person than me. I would have killed her in her sleep."

"Except she doesn't sleep, that we know of." Grey Cloak chuckled. "Don't worry. You won't get used to it. She's like sand and pebbles in your boots but much worse."

Zora reached over and touched his hand. "I'm glad you're here."

"Me too," he said, eyeballing the area. "I think."

Tanlin stretched out his arms and said, "I'm with Zora, and I want a bed. I'll secure some rooms. How many do I need?"

No one asked for a room.

"So one room for Zora and me. Not a problem at all, and it will save our chips."

"You don't want a room?" Zora asked Grey Cloak.

"I don't sleep much myself."

"Hmm, I suppose it's the human in me, but if you get tired, stop by the room, wherever that might be. The floor is yours."

"Thanks."

Tanlin secured a room in a tavern called The Squire's Post. It was a typical tavern with round tables on barrels surrounded by wooden captain's chairs. The chill air that swept down from the northern climates was muted by the warm fires of twin fireplaces on the far side of the tavern. The barkeep ran the tavern from behind the bar in the middle of the room. She was an older woman named Mona, husky and gray, with fire in her voice. Mona gave Tanlin the rundown.

"You can fight but no blades. Drink all that you want, and eat all you want, but whatever you break, you'll pay for." She slugged down a tankard of ale that she poured for herself. "Daggerford might not have the charm of Monarch City, but there are rules."

With his elbow on the bar, Tanlin asked casually, "And what might those be?"

"Well, I don't know them all. Use your common sense. You should know what you should and should not do. Sheesh." She flipped her dishrag over her shoulder and walked away. "Strangers."

Grey Cloak, Zora, Rhonna, and Lythlenion were sitting at the table. They were only a handful of the many hard-eyed patrons huddled over the tables of the smoky room.

Many of them were playing cards, rolling dice, talking coarsely, and drinking heartily.

"It looks like we aren't the only ones up this time of night," Lythlenion said as he covered his mouth and yawned.

An orc barmaid strolled over to the table with a tray of tankards. The ale sloshed over the rim of the mugs, and foam ran down the side. In a voice as gruff as Rhonna's, she said, "Daggerford is more awake in the night than in the day. Nothing but lazy cowards thrive here."

Lythlenion politely raised his hand and asked, "Um, could I get some coffee?"

The orcen barmaid batted her eyelashes at Lythlenion and said, "Say please, handsome."

He blushed and said, "Er... please?"

She winked at him and said, "I'll see what I can do. Anything else for the rest of you?" Before anyone could answer, she strutted away with her hips swinging like lanterns in the wind.

"I'm telling Sarah," Rhonna said as she sank her nose into her mug of ale.

"Who is Sarah?" Zora asked.

"My wife," Lythlenion said, "and I would never betray her."

Tanlin pushed his tankard over to Rhonna and said, "Good night, everyone. I'll see you in the morning."

"Yes, I'm going to turn in as well." Zora stood up and

brushed her hair over her shoulder. "Grey Cloak, I think you should get some rest. I think we all should. Stop by if you need to." She and Tanlin departed up the stairs.

Grey Cloak kept his eyes on Zora's figure, caught a fleeting good-night glance from her pretty eyes, and watched her disappear.

"You're too young for her," Rhonna said.

"Only by a few seasons. That's far from unheard of." He tried a sip of ale, and his nose crinkled. "You like this?"

"Not as much as what comes from Dwarf Skull. This isn't bitter enough."

"Bitter enough. It's bitter awful." He pushed the tankard away. "Help yourself to mine. All of it. I'm not thirsty, anyway."

The barmaid returned with a metal pot of coffee and poured it into a separate cup. "For you, sweet man," she said to Lythlenion and ran her fingers under his chin. "I'm Sammie. Try it."

"Of course." Lythlenion drank. "Mmm, it's very good. Good like my wife makes it."

"Then let your wife make the next pot." The barmaid picked up the pot and stormed away.

"Well done, smooth talker. Would it have killed you to flirt?" Rhonna asked. "Now we'll have to get our own drinks and food too."

"I didn't want her to get the wrong impression. It

wouldn't be fair to her, and it would dishonor Sarah," he answered.

Rhonna punched him in the arm. "I know. I was only fooling with you." She turned her attention to Grey Cloak. "But you, I wasn't fooling with. Watch out for women like Zora. You're barely a man."

"Barely a man is still a man," Grey Cloak replied.

Lythlenion gave an approving nod.

"Remember, I warned you. You want to save Dyphestive, then use your head and not your heart," Rhonna warned him. "There will be time enough to settle down later."

"Like you did?"

"Do I look like I'm settled down to you? Besides, I haven't met the right dwarf yet."

"Yes, you did," Lythlenion said. "Remember Jaargg Steelhand?"

"Hush it!" she said. If looks could kill, Lythlenion would be dead.

"Sorry, I shouldn't have—"

"Drop it," she replied. "Grey Cloak, trust me when I say, don't trust your heart. It can trip you. Keep a sharp mind instead."

"Good advice," Lythlenion agreed.

"I understand." He leaned back in his chair and said, "And believe me when I say that no woman is going to fool me."

The front door of the tavern opened, and the cold air brought in a gang of surly human men and women with cold, dead eyes. They sauntered into the tavern like they owned it. Weaponry jangled on their hips, and black whips with many tails showed prominently on two brawny men's corded forearms.

Grey Cloak sank down over the table. He'd heard of those men before. *The Scourge.*

42

"What are you huddled down in the floor for?" Rhonna asked as she gave Grey Cloak a funny look.

"I'm not in the floor," he said as he considered her point. He reached into his boot and shifted it on his foot. He wasn't sure why he'd shrunk either. Playing it off, he sat back up. "I think I still have pebbles in my boots."

The Scourge bumped every man and woman who was seated as they passed through the room. They made it pretty clear that they wanted to make their presence known. A mountain of a man with neck muscles up to his earlobes stared down four men seated at a large table in the back. The patrons jumped out of their seats, knocked them over, and hurried out of the tavern.

A woman of the Scourge with a long green ponytail tripped the last man on his way out. He hit the deck and crawled through the front door like a crab. The members of the Scourge tossed their heads back and let out obnoxious laughter.

"Drinks for my men! All of them!" a man who appeared to be the leader hollered. His hair was cut short, and he was long faced and had a square jaw and a voice like a lion. He, like most of the rest, wore scale-mail armor and had a black sash tied around his arms, showing off his bulging biceps. He pounded his mailed fist on the bar. "Drinks! Drinks! What does a man have to do to have a drink?"

The brusque waitress, Sammie, hurried over to him. "Your drinks are coming, Sash. There's no need to spook my customers."

"Do I look like a ghost?" In a fluid motion, Sash swung his arm over her back and grasped her wrist then reeled her in with a yank. "Mind yerself, Sammie. Or you'll serve, and we won't pay. Heh-heh. But lucky for you, tonight, we pay. We pay for all!" He slapped a small pile of chips on the bar. "Drink up, everyone, courtesy of the Scourge!"

Sammie pulled her arm away. "As you wish!" With a frown, she turned her back and started tapping the small barrels of ale. She hollered toward the back, "I need a hand out here!"

"They are a gutsy group, aren't they?" Lythlenion said.

"Yeah. Are you going to let them talk to your girl like that?" Rhonna replied.

"She's not my girl. I'm married."

Rhonna gave the slightest smile. She caught Sash's eye and lifted her tankard.

Sash nodded, swiped the first ale that Sammie poured, and headed to the back table with the rest of his brood.

Rhonna scratched her neck and asked Grey Cloak, "So you've heard of them?"

"Aye," he said, but his attention was elsewhere. He took a head count of the Scourge. There were five in all. Two men, Sash and the brute, were warriors, along with a woman clad the same as them. Another woman whose eyes constantly moved was wearing a winter cloak with fur on the collar. The last person was a bookish man, as bald as an onion, slight in build, with a nasty scar on his right cheek. He was warming his hands over the fire. He had tattoos, and rings covered his fingers.

"I've crossed them too," Rhonna said. She took a long drink and wiped her sleeve across her mouth. "Trouble-some adventurers. It was long ago, a different group, but all part of the same brand. And don't think for a moment that the ones that you see are all of them. I would bet my father's beard that more of them are outside, guarding whatever they found."

"Dragon charms," Grey Cloak said under his breath.

Lythlenion lowered his head and asked, "What do you mean?"

"The Scourge is after the same thing that Talon is... or was. Dragon charms. Tanlin and Browning told me about them." Grey Cloak looked over his shoulder at the group. The Scourge was in full celebration, slamming their tankards together and guzzling them down as fast as they could fill them. "Maybe they have one. Or more."

Rhonna's thick eyebrows furrowed. "I see that look in your eye, you little sneak. Now isn't the time to be nosey. We are this far north to find Dyphestive. That's the mission. No distractions."

"Fine, fine," he said in a reassuring manner. "But I don't think it would hurt to find out if they found one or not, would it? Maybe this is a gift."

"Look around," Rhonna warned. "If we took it... and that's assuming they have it... they would come right after us. Do you think we are equipped to take them on? Those are seasoned men and women. The Scourge is equipped with the best. I know that much. Keep your hands to yourself." She kicked his shin under the table.

"Ow!" he said. "Fine, I understand. I'll leave it alone. *For the moment.* At least let me go and tell Zora and Tanlin what is going on."

"I have an idea. Go up there and stay there," Rhonna suggested.

"As you wish." He quickly got up from his chair and headed for the steps.

The green-haired woman from the Scourge stepped into his path. "Where do you think you are going, handsome?"

43

The brash woman had caught Grey Cloak off guard, and his tongue couldn't find any words. He was captured by her calculating eyes, which were searching his. Finally, he managed to say, "Uh... upstairs?"

She turned and looked up the staircase. "Why do you want to go up there? The fun is down here."

He faked a yawn. "I'm very tired."

"You don't look very tired to me," she said in a sultry voice. She offered her hand. "I'm Katrina."

He shook her hand. She had a very strong grip. "Grey Cloak," he said.

Katrina didn't release his hand and said, "Funny name but catchy. I like it." She was a well-knit warrior, rugged but pretty in her own way and noticeably shapely in her scale armor. Her long green hair showed natural brown roots. It was combed straight back into a single pony tail.

"Why don't you have a drink with me, Grey Cloak? I could use your company. It's been a very long day, and I'm celebrating."

He swallowed the lump building in his throat. "I really shouldn't, and I'm not very good company or much of a drinker."

"That's too bad." She offered him a playful smile and released her grip. "If you change your mind, you know where to find me."

"Uh... thank you." He started up the stairs.

Katrina swatted him on the behind. "See you around, Grey Cloak."

He hurried up the steps and glanced at Rhonna and Lythlenion. They were looking at him and laughing. He continued up the stairs and knocked on Tanlin's door.

Zora opened the door and smiled the moment she saw him. "Well, isn't this a surprise? Please, come in, night owl."

Tanlin was already tucked in one of the twin beds with a cloth nightcap on his head.

"Really? You are in bed so soon?" Grey Cloak asked.

"The older you get, the more you'll learn to appreciate the simple pleasures of life," Tanlin replied. He made a curious expression and scooted up into a sitting position. "Judging by the look on your face, I take it you have *bad* news?"

"Possibly." Grey Cloak sat down on the other twin bed.

Zora seated herself by him. "What is it?"

"Shortly after you came up here, another group entered the tavern. It's the Scourge."

Tanlin's eyes widened. "How do you know this?"

"Black tattoos, and they toasted themselves as *the Scourge.*"

"What did they look like? What did they say?" Tanlin asked urgently.

"The leader's name is Sash."

Tanlin and Zora exchanged uneasy looks.

He slid his nightcap off and crumpled it over his chest. "Who else?"

"The only other name I know was a woman I met named Katrina. She slapped me on my rear end."

Zora stiffened. "She did what?"

He smirked. "Jealous?"

"Hah," she replied.

Grey Cloak continued, "There was another warrior, as big as a horse, a skin-headed wizard, and a woman whose eyes seemed to rattle around in her skull." He leaned forward. "I take it you know them?"

"Yes, I've crossed paths with them more than once," Tanlin said. His silky speech became bitter. "Needless to say, we aren't on friendly terms, nor will we ever be."

"Care to elaborate?"

"No." Tanlin sat up and swung his legs out from underneath the covers. "What else?"

"Nothing, really. They are celebrating. Sash is buying ale for everyone. That's why I came up here. Perhaps there is an opportunity here."

Zora gave him a curious look and asked, "What is going on between those pointed ears of yours?"

"Well, perhaps they have a dragon charm. Perhaps we could steal it," he suggested.

Tanlin ran a narrow finger under his lips. "Hmm, did you run this by Rhonna?"

"Yes, she hates the idea. She wants us to stay on point."

"I can't blame her there," Zora said.

"Still, we are Talon, and we hate the Scourge. I wouldn't mind taking a crack at sticking a thorn in their backsides. They've done us in more than once. Interesting." Tanlin reached across and placed a hand on Zora's knee. "We can't let them see us."

"I know they can't see you, but they've never seen me," she said. "So were there only five?"

"Perhaps more are outside, Rhonna said," Grey Cloak replied. He was surprised that Tanlin and Zora were getting on board so quickly. He'd expected the opposite. Perhaps that was because Dalsay and Adanadel were normally in control and the pair of thieves was more open to stealing.

Tanlin blew out the candles in the room. "Let's take a peek outside, shall we." He raised the window and pushed open the shutters. Across the street were stables, and two men in heavy cloaks and scale armor were standing guard. "It looks like they are packing something valuable. Treasure, perhaps."

"What about a dragon charm? How would they carry that if they had one?" Grey Cloak asked.

"They would keep it on one of them or in a strongbox, perhaps. They've acquired many," Tanlin said. "We need to learn more about it." He opened a wooden chest at the end of his bed and took his folded clothing out. "Zora and I will take a peek in the barn."

"And what am I going to do?"

"Go make nice with your friend Katrina. Squeeze out more information," Tanlin said as he slipped out of his nightgown and into his shirt.

Grey Cloak started for the door.

Zora hooked his arm. "Don't get too nice."

44

"Have you ever been to Daggerford before?" Katrina asked as she brushed Grey Cloak's hair back over his ear.

"No, first time." He was sitting beside her on a stool with his back to the bar. It gave him a full view of the tavern. To his surprise, Rhonna and Lythlenion had joined the Scourge at the table in the back. They were playing cards, and Rhonna was smoking a cigar. "What about you?"

"I've been just about everywhere in Gapoli." She ran her fingers through his jet-black hair. "I hope you can forgive my fascination, but I envy elves. They have the finest features, and yours are particularly astounding. Oh, I wish I had hair like yours."

He gave her green locks a casual glance and said, "Yours is very nice. Uh, pretty."

She laughed and slapped him on the back. "You flatter me but don't do a good job. I'm covered in the grit of the road and smell like horses and rotten men. But you are kind. I can see it in your eyes." Katrina drank from her tankard. "Tell me, are you from Arrowwood?"

Grey Cloak squirmed. "Er, no, Portham, actually," he lied but quickly shifted the focus back to her. "And you?" He turned on the charm. "Let me guess. Monarch City?"

"Maybe, maybe not. Are you sure that you wouldn't like some of my ale?" She'd begun to slur her *s*'s. "One little drink—Sash is buying."

"To be honest, I'd like to, but it sours my stomach." He shrugged. "I guess I don't have a palate for it, unlike my friends."

Katrina rolled her neck toward the table of card players. "Oh, them. Strange company that you keep."

"Really? How so?"

"You're handsome, and they are not." She giggled, reached down, and peeled his cloak open. "So what brings you to Daggerford? Hmm. Why are you packing steel?"

"One can't be too careful when they travel," he said.

"True. You never know when you might run across brigands—or worse, someone like us."

The mountain of a man slammed his fist on the card table then stood up and jabbed a finger at Rhonna. "Cheater!" he said in a voice that lacked deep intelligence.

Rhonna puffed on her cigar and raked a small pile of coins her way. She had a sliver of delight in her stony face.

"Sit down, Bull," Sash warned. "Those are fighting words. And we aren't here to fight." He nodded at Rhonna. "We are here to gamble. If you don't like the outcome, you can leave the table."

The brute glared at Rhonna and plopped down in his chair.

"Bull is horrible at cards. Sash tells him not to play, but he doesn't listen. When it's just us, we have to let him win sometimes to keep him happy. After all, he is the strongest man in Westerlund. He's good to have around," Katrina said. "Now, where were we?"

Grey Cloak shifted her focus away from him, played dumb, and said, "I don't recall, but perhaps you could tell me what you are celebrating. You never told me that."

"Ah-ah-ah-ah," she said as she waggled her finger in his face. "What do you take me for? Some loose-lipped wench?"

"Certainly not. I was only curious, and well, Sash seemed rather boastful about it. After all, he's buying round after round."

Reeking with ale, she got nose to nose with him and asked, "What do you think we did?"

"You are adventurers, and you found treasure in a lost tomb of some sort?"

She nodded and leaned back. "We are the Scourge. Haven't you ever heard of us?"

"No, but after tonight, I'll never forget. That much is certain." *Keep her talking.* "Have you been a member of the Scourge long?"

"You ask a lot of questions."

"I'm only making conversation. I thought that was what you wanted." He turned on the charm and smiled. "And you are very interesting. A strong woman, a world traveler, possibly a slayer of countless horrors, let alone very attractive. That's why I came back down. I wanted to learn more about you."

"That's pretty thick," she said, breathing heavily, "but I like it. I think I'll let you get away with it. But I've hurt men for less."

"Well, I'm not a man. I'm an elf."

"True, but a young one. I must have fifteen seasons on you."

"I wouldn't have guessed more than five."

Katrina blushed. "You're good. I know that you don't mean it, but I still like it."

Grey Cloak got comfortable, turned toward her, and put his elbow on the bar. *It's working. Time to pour it on.* "Tell me more about you and the Scourge. You know you want to. And I'm curious."

Katrina's lips twitched. She might have had a hard shell, but she was human, and her defenses were lowered. She glanced at the front door and back at the card table. Only Sash, Bull, Rhonna, and Lythlenion were playing. The other two members of the Scourge, the woman with a fur collar on her cloak and the skin-headed lizard-faced wizard, were sitting at their own table. No one was paying attention to Katrina. She tugged on her hoop earrings. "I've been in the Scourge for over ten seasons. Started up with Sash. We've been called a lot of things over the years. Mercenaries, freebooters, brigands, adventurers, tomb raiders, monster slayers, dragon hunters—"

"Dragon hunters?"

She gave him a crafty-eyed look and nodded. "Aye. I've seen it all and lived to tell about it." She patted the pommel of the well-crafted sword on her hip. "Because I'm that good."

"No doubt."

"Squirrel," Sash called suddenly.

The busy-eyed woman turned and met his gaze. Her brown hair was short and messy. She spoke quickly. "What? What do you wish?"

"Head outside. Check on your henchmen and gear. Make sure everything is all right."

"Yes, right away, Sash," Squirrel said. She lifted herself out of her chair, weaved through the tables like a little varmint, and went out the door.

Grey Cloak braced his head against his hand. *Oh no, Tanlin and Zora are out there!*

45

Zora and Tanlin slipped out of the tavern and waited in the shadows of the streets of Daggerford. From across the street, they watched the two henchmen that were posted outside of the stables. The men stood tall in the cold air, with their cloaks wrapped tight around their shoulders. A small wood fire was burning in a metal urn that stood between them.

"Do you recognize them?" she asked.

"No. They are retainers. But we need to be sure that no one else is lurking about." Tanlin's eyes followed a small group of people hurrying down the road. The henchmen's shoulders turned toward the passersby. "They take the job seriously. I would say that they are guarding something worth taking a peek at. I'll distract them while you go around back and see if you can find another way to squeeze in."

Zora nodded and hurried down the alley, passed a few buildings, and crossed the road. Making her way down the alley, she peeked around the corner at the rear of the stables. She didn't see anyone at the back of the row of buildings that faced the countryside. With her shoulder almost brushing the back walls of the buildings, she crept toward the stable.

A figure-like lump was huddled at the back of the stable, the orange glow of a cigar end burning, and a stream of smoke rose into the air. *Dragon dung!*

The burning cigar end turned in Zora's direction. She sank into a crouch and pressed her body against the wall.

A man stretched his neck out and stood. His body rose higher and higher. The tall and skinny henchman walked in long, slow strides toward Zora. A dagger scraped out of its sheath.

Zooks! He's coming right at me! He couldn't have seen me. I'm better than that.

The henchman walked right by her and peered around the bend of the same wooden building. He looked back and forth and scratched his head, scanning the fields. Then he walked back toward the stable, stopped right in front of her, faced the fields, and smoked. "Ah, I hate this stuff," he muttered.

Good. Now, go away. The back was guarded, and that

was all she needed to turn around and go. They would have to abandon the plan of seeing what the Scourge possessed. It wasn't worth the risk. *Move on so I can get out of the cold and rest my head.*

The man turned halfway around and started to step toward the stable but stopped. He looked straight at her and squatted. "The sad thing is that I didn't see you or hear you." He reached out and pushed her hood away from her face. "I smelled you. It was the odor of the smoke and incense that's stuck on you." Using his dagger's tip, he lifted her chin. "Well, well, well, isn't this pleasant a surprise. A pretty little flower."

She gave him a quaint smile. "Good evening."

"Yes, indeed." He kept the tip of his dagger on her throat. "Up now."

She rose and didn't take her eyes of him.

"What is your name, little flower?" he asked.

"Zora."

"Zora, I am Hawk." He had thick eyebrows and the eyes of a predator. The direness in his tone made him a man not to be trifled with.

"Tell me," he said, "what are you doing here?"

"Passing through, taking a walk. What are you doing?"

"Standing guard. And for good reason, it seems. It looks like I found a weasel in the hen house." He took a quick look from side to side. "How long have you been following us?"

"Not long," she said.

"Hah, I know better than that." He took off her belt of daggers. "I know a thief when I see one. Regardless, I'd better let Sash know that I sniffed you out. This should be adequate enough to get me out of the doghouse with him. Hands up. March."

She slowly lifted her hands and said, "Speaking of sniffing, sniff this." She swiped her ring finger under his nose. A latch opened on the ring's flat setting, and a fine mist burst into Hawk's face.

Hawk inhaled, and his nostrils flared. He spat out, "You dirty little minx..." Then he collapsed on the ground.

"Yep, that's me, a dirty little minx that dropped a hawk." She stepped over him. The ring's mist would have him out cold for hours. She hooked his arms and dragged him to the back of the stable and propped him up against the wall. *And with any luck, he won't remember a thing.*

The ring of mist had a few unpredictable powers. Depending on the person, not only would they sleep, but they could lose their most recent memories as well. However, in some cases, it had the opposite effect, making a person bright-eyed and bushy-tailed, hostile, and angry.

At the back of the large stables was a small door big enough for chickens to crawl through. On her hands and knees, she squeezed her half-elf body through the portal. She stood up and dusted the hay off of her clothing. Some of it had stuck to her. "Yuck."

Zora hustled toward the front. Tanlin was talking to the henchmen and warming his hands over the fire. *Perfect.*

She moved from stable to stable, eyeing the big horses that the Scourge was known for riding. Inside one of the stalls, there wasn't a horse at all, but a wagon. It had a hump in the middle and was covered with canvas. *This must be it.*

Quietly, Zora opened the gate to the stall and stepped inside. Using her agile hands, she rolled up the canvas and shoved it back, revealing an iron cage.

She jerked her hand away with a sharp gasp. A dragon as big as a sheepdog was inside the cage. Its fiery-pink eyes were locked on Zora's and took her breath away. *I can't move!*

46

"Is something wrong?" Katrina asked Grey Cloak.

He fanned his hand in front of his face and said, "Sometimes the smoke gets to me, and I need a breath of fresh air. Do you mind?"

"Not at all. I could use a breath of fresh air myself. It's getting stuffy in here."

"No, I could also use a spot of privacy." He hopped off his barstool and pulled away her grip that she'd fastened on his cloak. "I need to, well, you know, relieve myself, quickly."

"But you haven't had a bit to drink."

He backed toward the front door. "True, but I'm known for holding my water all day. Sometimes for two days. I'll return shortly." He backed out the door into the cool of the night.

Outside, Squirrel had already scurried across the street and was talking to the henchmen. Tanlin was there, as well, but he kept his face hidden from Squirrel and moved on. When he caught Grey Cloak's eyes, he gave a subtle wave, signaling for Grey Cloak to go back inside.

Squirrel entered the stables and vanished in the darkness. *Horseshoes!*

He stepped off the tavern porch and into the alley. The wary henchmen watched him. He moved back into the shadows. In the cover of darkness, he kept his eye on the stable entrance.

Tanlin snuck up behind him from the back of the alley. "What are you doing here?" he whispered.

"I saw Squirrel go out and thought I'd better warn you," he said. "Where's Zora?"

"I don't know. She went around to the back. I've been working the front. She could be in there."

"Do you know Squirrel? Is she dangerous?"

"Zora can handle herself. Don't worry about her. Get back inside, though. I can handle this." He tied a royal-blue scarf around his neck and shoved Grey Cloak in the back. "Go."

Grey Cloak jumped onto the porch. As soon as he did, Katrina came out.

"There you are," she said. "I was beginning to miss you."

He spread his arms out in a friendly gesture. "Here I am."

"I can see that." She rubbed her shoulders. "Come inside. It's cold out here." She wrapped her arm around his waist. "I desire the warmth of your company."

Squirrel emerged from the stables and hustled across the street. "Kat," she said in an edgy voice. "A word."

"Can't you see I have company?"

"Yes, you always have company. If he was smart, he would run." Squirrel jumped on the porch. "This is business."

"Tell Sash."

"Of course. I'll tell him, and he'll wonder why I didn't tell you. That won't go well." Squirrel pulled the handle on the door.

Katrina pushed the door shut. With an eye roll, she asked, "What is it?"

"Business." Squirrel shooed Grey Cloak away. "Do you mind?"

"No," Grey Cloak said.

Squirrel made her point clear when a dagger magically appeared in her hand and she pointed it in his face. "Go... away."

He stepped off the porch near the alley and said, "I'll wait over here." There was no sign of Tanlin, but he did see the slightest footprint impressions going across the road.

I'll be. He's invisible. That clever old fox. The prints went right behind the henchmen and into the alley.

Katrina turned her head toward the stables. "I'll check it out. Tell Sash and Honzur." She started across the street.

Oh no, I have to stop her!

47

Grey Cloak jumped into Katrina's path and stopped her. "Is something wrong? I can help you."

"Little elf, you're fine company, but this is business." She pushed through him.

"I'll come and help."

She stopped and said, "No, you wait here."

"But I have my own horse in there. Not to be rude, but I have as much reason to be in there as you. Did someone steal your horse?"

"No. Bloody barons, will you *go on*?"

"Of course." He sprinted right between the two hench-men, and into the stable he went.

"Grey Cloak!" she yelled after him.

He grabbed a lantern as he entered and turned up the

flame. He offered it to Katrina when she caught up with him. "See? I told you that I could be helpful."

"Keep the lantern up and come with me." She led him to the stables at the back of the barn. One of the stall gates was open in the back, and a wagon covered in canvas was inside. "I don't see anyone. Has Squirrel gone crazy?"

"She *looks* crazy." He pointed at his eyes. "They move a lot." He lifted the canvas and asked, "What is in here?"

She smacked his hand away. "Do you want to get yourself killed? Do that again, and I'll cut your fingers off."

He hid his free hand behind his back and said, "I wouldn't want that. It would make clapping nearly impossible."

Squirrel stormed into the stables followed by Sash, Bull, and Honzur. Rhonna and Lythlenion drifted in behind them.

"What did you do with her, Kat?" Squirrel demanded.

"No one was here," Katrina said.

"I tied her to this post! And now you're telling me that she's gone?" Squirrel said.

"I didn't see anyone," Grey Cloak said. "Perhaps you didn't tie a very good knot."

"What is he doing here?" Sash demanded.

"It's fine. He came in with me," Katrina said.

"He let her go!" Squirrel said.

"No, he didn't!" Katrina said.

Squirrel frantically jabbed a finger at Katrina. "Do you

see what she does? Every time we come across a comely elf, she gets out of sorts."

"I do not!" she shouted in Squirrel's face. "And maybe if we let an elf in the group, it wouldn't be an issue."

"Stitch your holes! Both of you!" Sash ordered.

The women fell silent.

"First off..." The rangy, fish-eyed warrior pointed at Grey Cloak, Rhonna, and Lythlenion. "You, you, and you need to get your noses out of our business."

"I have as much a right to be here as you," Rhonna said. "My horses and gear are in this barn, and I'm not going anywhere until I check them."

In his dumb voice, Bull said, "Did someone steal the dragon?"

Sash faced Bull, glaring at him. He reached up and clamped his hand over Bull's mouth, and his fingers dug into the brute's cheeks. "What did I tell you about talking?"

Bull shrugged and said through Sash's fingers, "Don't do it?"

"A dragon, huh? Not our concern," Rhonna said as she and Lythlenion backed away. The henchmen blocked their path to the exit.

"Not so fast," Sash said. "Seeing how the cat is out of the bag, you might as well stay."

The mage, Honzur, shuffled over to the wagon. Though he had a fragile build, he had strength in his eyes. His colorful tattooed hands and fingers lifted the canvas from the cage.

A dragon the size of a retriever was sitting inside the cage. Its scales were like ivory, and its eyes were fiery pink.

"The dragon is secure," Honzur said, "yet I still sense a presence."

"That's because someone else was in here. A part elf. A woman. Auburn hair," Squirrel said. Her shifty gaze darted all over the barn. "She couldn't have gotten far."

"Hawk!" Sash hollered. "Hawk! Where is that slack-jawed fool? Something smells rotten. Bull, go out back and find him." He eyed Rhonna. "You wouldn't know anything about this, would you, dwarf?"

"Apparently, I know as much as you," Rhonna said.

"Don't take me for a fool. I can tell by your grit that you've seen a scrap or two. What's your story?"

"That's none of your concern."

Sash pulled out his sword. It had an ivory handle and a one-sided black blade. "Stay put. The rest of you, search this barn. From top to bottom. Now."

Grey Cloak followed Katrina.

"Not you!" Sash said. "Get over here with these two."

Lythlenion lifted a finger and said, "This is hardly a way to treat new acquaintances."

"Stitch it, Blondie." Sash kept his sword on them while Katrina and Squirrel ducked in and out of the stalls.

Bull returned, carrying a tall and lean man in his arms.

"He's dead," Bull said with a sniffle. "Hawk's dead."

Hawk's chest was still rising and falling.

"He's not dead. He's asleep." Sash slapped Hawk's face several times. "Wakey-wakey! Bloody barons, he's out stone cold." He eyed Talon. "This has your stink all over it."

"Don't look at us. We've been in your presence the whole time," Rhonna said. "Methinks you were tired of losing."

"I would have won my chips back. I always do."

Grey Cloak noticed Honzur standing in front of a head-high pile of straw. It was the perfect place to hide. The wizard's right hand began to glow with azure energy, and a wind swept through the stables. The horses whinnied and bucked inside their stalls.

Sash shielded his eyes. "What are you doing, Honzur?"

The pile of straw began to funnel and spin then rose from the ground like a spinning cloud, scattering straw all over the barn and revealing two bodies hiding within. It was Tanlin cradling Zora.

The fire in Honzur's hands died down, and the swirling winds along with it. Grey Cloak inched toward Zora, who was lying in Tanlin's arms in a catatonic state. Rhonna seized his elbow.

"Don't let them go anywhere, Bull," Sash said as he strolled alongside Honzur. "Well, well, well, who do we have here? My, oh my, it looks like Tanlin. And where Tanlin is, Talon can't be far behind."

48

"Get up!" Sash said with a flick of his sword blade. "Squirrel, is this the woman you saw?"

"Yes," Squirrel said.

"Good, we are making progress."

Tanlin stood and glared hatefully at Sash.

"Don't look at me like that. The death of Jeena wasn't my fault," Sash said. He rested his sword on his shoulder. "It's in the past. Move on."

"It's not in the past. I live it every day," Tanlin said with his voice cracking.

Grey Cloak had never seen Tanlin so distraught. It was so far out of character that it rattled him.

"And if Jeena had died at the hands of a chimera or a harpy, you could have lived with that, but because I allegedly had something to do with it, you hold a grudge against me." Sash smoothed his hand over his short hair. "You need to move on."

"She died drowning. I was seconds from saving her. You let it happen," Tanlin said.

"I thought you would save her. I was only buying time. What do you want? An apology?" Sash bowed. "I'm sorry. Feel better."

"You are scum," Tanlin said.

"Speaking of scum, where are the unflappable Dalsay and Adanadel lurking? I can only imagine that they put you up to this," Sash said. "Squirrel, take a closer look about, will you?" He dusted straw off of his shoulder. "Well, Tanlin?"

"They aren't here," Tanlin responded.

Grey Cloak noticed the wizard, Honzur, touching the ugly slash mark on his cheek.

"Am I to take it that you alone—well, you and this girl, possibly them too"—he pointed his sword at Grey Cloak —"are robbing me on your own? That would be foolish, and I know that you aren't foolish."

Honzur wrung his hands, and with his eyes rolled up in his head, he said, "I don't have a sense of Dalsay. Or see any others." He dabbed his forehead with his sleeve and took a breath. "Interesting. However, I can't always sense them, or the presence of magic used by the Wizard Watch." His eyes darted around as if something in the shadows might attack him. "We are clear of it, for the moment."

Grey Cloak remembered Browning's story about the horror that the Figurine of Heroes summoned. The warrior had said that the one-eyed imp monster attacked Honzur. *I bet that is where he got that ugly scar from.*

Sash pointed his sword at Tanlin's chest. "Where are they? Don't dally with me, Tanlin. You know I will hurt you —you and your young friend."

"I have no doubt about that," Tanlin said.

Grey Cloak eyed the scarf on Tanlin's neck. He assumed it was what Tanlin had used to make himself invisible. *Why doesn't he use it? Escape.*

Tanlin stepped in front of Zora and said, "It gives me no pleasure to reveal this to you, of all people, but Dalsay and Adanadel are dead."

"Hah! Do you really expect me to believe that?" Sash marched back and forth, eyeing the rafters. He spun on his heel. "I always fantasized about killing Adanadel myself. He was one of the finest swordsmen, but now, well, how did they die? Spiked pit? Dragon fire? The touch of the undead? Come now, I want details."

"Doom Riders," Tanlin replied.

"You're joking. Doom Riders, Black Frost's most powerful henchmen. Hah! Only the Riskers are greater." Sash scratched at the stubble on his chin. "How did all of this come about?"

"Wrong place. Wrong time. Certainly, you can understand the outcome when evil encounters the good."

"Yes, evil will run it over, at least in the Doom Riders' case. Hah, I strive to be one myself, but apparently, my abilities are not perfect enough." Sash dropped his hand onto Tanlin's shoulder. "Did you see it?"

"I came upon it after the deed. They lay dead in the streets of Raven Cliff."

"What happened to Dalsay?" Honzur asked.

"His body was filled with crossbow bolts."

"Drysis!" Sash said with admiration. "Ah, I've met her once. She's a goddess of war. I would give my left arm to ride a gourn with her."

Honzur shuffled over to Tanlin. "Where is Dalsay's body?"

"Tatiana took him to the Wizard Watch. That is all that I know of it. Adanadel was returned to Monarch City, and Browning is buried in the dead fields of Raven Cliff."

"Browning is gone, too, huh?" Sash nodded. "I liked him. Was a better fit for the Scourge than Talon. Oh well, at least he died an honorable death, which is more than what I can say for you. Are there any others?"

"No. You'll be happy to know Talon is dead. Our meeting is a coincidence."

Sash cocked his head and said, "Oh, I don't think so. Your girl tried to steal my dragon."

"She is young and only curious," Tanlin replied.

Squirrel returned. "There isn't any sign of anyone else,

Sash. But I did manage to dig up some more pertinent information."

Sash rolled his hand and said, "Well, spit it out. No need to keep us lingering."

"I spoke to the tavern dwellers and found out that all of them"—she pointed at the members of Talon—"arrived together. I confirmed it with Sammie."

"Is that so?" He gave Rhonna a foreboding look. "Let me guess. You are the new members of Talon. Hah. And there is only one warrior among you at that. Tsk. Tsk. Tsk. What were you thinking, Tanlin? That you could lead this group without heavy steel? Hah. Honzur, Squirrel, string them up to the posts."

"They are innocent in all of this," Tanlin argued. "I hardly know them. We met them on the trail."

"Hah!" Sash shoved Tanlin to the ground and picked up Zora by the hair. "We'll see how well everyone knows everyone. This one is charmed. It will be a peaceful way to die."

"Let her go!" Grey Cloak said. He'd kept his lip buttoned up long enough. He needed to buy time. And he couldn't bear to watch Zora die, not like that. Enough had died already. "We are together. Just don't kill her. Not like that. What do you want from us?"

"I want Talon out of my life, once and for all," Sash said. "I can't have you coming between my rewards and status."

"We won't," Tanlin promised. "I swear this is a coincidence."

"How so?" Sash asked. "You keep saying that, but how? And don't try to fool me, Tanlin. My deck is stacked."

Rhonna and Lythlenion were disarmed and seated, tied to a post by Squirrel. Tanlin was rough-handled by the henchmen and tied to another post with Grey Cloak by Katrina.

"I'm disappointed," Katrina whispered in Grey Cloak's ear. "You deceived me. You'll wish that you hadn't. Sad, too... you might have fit the Scourge like a glove."

After they were all tied up, Honzur made his rounds. His tattooed fingers had webbing all over them. He tied the sticky webbing all over Talon's bonds, making the knots impossible to loosen.

Sash tied Zora up and placed her body in the wagon with the dragon.

"What are you doing with her?" Tanlin asked.

"Tanlin, I feel sorry for you. You lost your wife, and the truth is, I feel bad." Sash touched his heart and nodded. "I'm not without a heart. So I'll spare this one. Perhaps, when she comes to her senses and realizes that she has nothing left, she'll join us." He eyed Katrina. "Get the horses out. All of them. Honzur, settle the dragon. It's going to be a long trip."

Honzur was standing at the end of the wagon. He removed a fiery-pink gemstone the size of an egg from his pocket. The dragon's intense eyes locked on it. Wherever Honzur moved his hand, the dragon's head followed. The wizard muttered arcane words quietly, and the dragon sank down in his cage and slept.

"It is done," Honzur said as he placed the dragon charm in his pocket. "The crypt dragon is under my complete control. Black Frost will be pleased with this find. This dragon's unique abilities are binding. The girl won't wake until the dragon tells her to."

"Good. Tell me, Tanlin, what is the girl's name?"

With his head down, Tanlin replied, "Zora."

"I like it. Perhaps we will keep her if she learns to behave." He watched his company lead the horses out of the stables. Bull grabbed the wagon by the hitch and rolled it out on his own. "Change of plans. Tonight, we ride to the Dark Ridges. Squirrel, burn the barn. And make sure our old friends can't escape."

"They won't," Honzur assured him.

"That's it? You're going to burn us to death?" Rhonna wrestled with her sticky bindings. "You coward!"

"I'm not going to burn you to death. Squirrel is," Sash said as he backed away from the barn. Every person and beast was out of the barn except for Squirrel. "Nice meeting all of you. Normally, I would say 'Until we meet again,' but it's highly unlikely that will happen. May your burning bones fertilize your unknown grave. Goodbye, Talon."

Using the oil lanterns, Squirrel hurried through the

stables, setting small fires by busting the lanterns all over the stalls. The fire devoured the centuries-old dry wood. The smoke began to spread. She winked at Grey Cloak as she passed by, then she left the stables and closed the door behind her.

49

G rey Cloak prided himself on being able to escape anything, but the more he moved his fingers, the stickier they became. He wasn't going anywhere. "I'm sorry, all. This is my fault."

"You think?" Rhonna blurted. "I told you what not to do, and did you listen? No. You have to learn patience."

"I said I was sorry."

"A fat lot of good that is going to do us now!" she said. A ring of flames reflected in her eyes.

Tanlin started coughing. "It's not all his fault. I jumped into this feet first too. I should have known better."

"But you're thieves. The lot of you," Rhonna stated. "And you can't help yourself, any more than a scorpion striking. So tell me, Grey Cloak, with all of us dead, who is going to save Dyphestive?"

Grey Cloak had gotten so caught up in his ambitions that he'd forgotten all about his blood brother. And that wasn't all that he was responsible for. *Zora. I've doomed her as well.* He tried rubbing his wrists up and down the post, hoping to catch a sharp edge of something, but the webbing held fast. The smoke started stinging his eyes, and the heat caused his face to break out in new sweat. "Tanlin, tell me you have something."

"No, I can't say that I do," Tanlin replied in his calm and collected voice, "aside from an ever-growing hatred for Sash. You know, he used to be one of us."

"Really?"

"Adanadel booted him out. He said his heart was wicked. Not all of us agreed, but Adanadel was proved right when Sash killed Tatiana's brothers and my wife. It was the ultimate betrayal."

"Thanks for the history lesson, but that isn't going to help us get out of these flames," Rhonna said. She blew at the fires eating up the hay and licking at her boots. "Talk about something else. Pray for rain, why don't you? Lyth, any ideas?"

The orc coughed and said, "Silence. That would help. I'm trying to utter a protection spell, but it won't do much good if I lose my concentration."

"You heard him. Seal your lips!" Rhonna said.

Grey Cloak clammed up, and words loaded with mysticism began rolling off of Lythlenion's tongue. A stiff cough broke his rhythm.

"Horseshoes!" He started again.

"You can do it," Rhonna said. Her already-ruddy skin had reddened even further. "Concentrate."

Grey Cloak began choking on the suffocating heat and smoke. He felt like he was in the fire himself. The roar of the flames began to rise all around him. The posts and stalls were aflame.

If I could only get the Figurine of Heroes out. Perhaps my cloak has another ability. He concentrated on what he desired. He wanted the figurine to worm its way out of his pockets and wished for the flames to go out. Nothing happened.

"Hurry, Lythlenion, please," Tanlin said. Sweat dripped off of his chin. He rolled his neck from side to side and started a fit of coughing. "Never imagined I would die like this."

"You aren't dead yet. None of us is. Keep fighting," Rhonna said.

Tanlin droned on desperately. "How do you fight a fire? No water. No nothing."

The fire ran across the roof and rafters. The old wood popped and crackled, and the flames roared with ravenous life.

This entire place is going to be nothing in a few more seconds. The fire drowned out Lythlenion's voice. His watery eyes couldn't see the cleric or Rhonna through the smoke. A large beam in the ceiling collapsed, and the roof started to fall in chunks. *This is it!* The stable collapsed all around them.

RESIDENTS MADE a chain of buckets and tossed water onto the fire, but the effort was futile.

Sash was sitting on his horse, watching the stables burn in a great pillar of flame. "Well done, Squirrel. Well done, everyone." Sash tapped his chest and chin and made a circle around it. "I mourn for my enemies as I mourn for my men." He turned his horse north. With the flames and people praying for mercy at their backs, the Scourge thundered out of town.

50

Darkness. Searing heat. Grey Cloak choked on ashes that spilled into his mouth. He couldn't see a thing.

Strong hands pulled him out of the smoldering black, and he gasped and coughed fiercely.

"Breathe, boy, breathe!" Rhonna said. She had her strong arms hooked underneath his armpits, and she dragged him through the cinders and into the street.

Grey Cloak moved onto his hands and knees and coughed himself hoarse. His mouth tasted like he'd eaten logs out of a fireplace. He spat on the ground and sucked in the cool night air. "What happened? How are we alive?"

"Lythlenion pulled through," Rhonna said then cleared her throat and spit. She was covered in ashes from head to toe. He couldn't see the skin on her face. "He usually does."

Grey Cloak wiped the grit from his eyes. Lythlenion

was patting Tanlin on the back, and the older rogue was sitting down with his head between his knees.

"I can't believe we are still alive. I started to think I wasn't going to survive." He let out a sigh.

Rhonna helped him to his feet. "You can't think like that. Ever."

"I know. But recently, it seems I've been on the losing end of things. It's time to turn that around." He set his eyes north. "They've gone ahead, you believe?"

"I can't say. I only dug myself out of the ashes a moment before I pulled you out." She dusted off her garb. "I hope you'll be wise enough to listen to me from here on out. No more risk."

He nodded.

Sammie the bartender rushed across the street with a wool blanket then threw it over Lythlenion's shoulders and hugged him tight. "Thank the seasons you are still alive, my dearest. I take back the harsh words I said. Let me care for you."

"Thank you for the sentiment, but I have a wife to care for me." He gently brushed her aside and handed her the blanket. "And I'm still very warm, inside and out."

Sammie frowned as she drew her blanket to her chest. "You have a blessed wife. I can't help but be jealous. Those men, the Scourge, they're already riding toward the Dark Ridges, but they don't have much of a head start on you."

"They don't even need a head start. They have our

horses and our weapons," Rhonna said. She kicked the ashes at her feet and looked at Grey Cloak. "Well done."

"We'll get them back. I promise."

Rhonna huffed.

RHONNA LED THE MARCH NORTH, clearly in a somber mood. It wasn't much different for the rest of them. Using all of the coins they had left, they'd bought rations, one horse, and an assortment of suitable weapons. They moved all night long, hoping to keep pace with the Scourge.

The plan was simple: rescue Zora. Grey Cloak was determined to do it. Her capture was his fault, and he was going to take responsibility. It was the least he could do for his friend. Plus, he could do without Rhonna's bitter faces and replies every time he talked to her.

They moved all night long and into the morning, not stopping, until they could see the Dark Ridges in the far distant northern horizon. Rhonna was leading, a weary Tanlin was stooped over the horse's saddle horn, and Grey Cloak was in the rear with Lythlenion.

"I never thanked you for saving my life. Our lives." He offered his hand. "Thank you."

Lythlenion gave a pleasant smile and said, "My pleasure. The truth is, even I thought we weren't going to make it. The smoke and heat fouled up my incantation, but my flame screen spell ignited in the nick of time. Heh. That was a close one. But the only things I could think of were my Sarah and my daughter, Lylith." He put a firm hand on Grey Cloak's shoulder. "Don't let Rhonna get to you. She's a grump but secretly delights in it."

"That explains a lot about the misery she put me through," Grey Cloak joked. He eyeballed a mace that Lythlenion was carrying. Its craftsmanship was poor compared to the war mace he'd carried before. "You've lost your weapon too. I'll help you get it back."

"You are ambitious, but my war mace, Thunderash, is only a weapon, not a person. Don't expect so much of yourself. Keep it simple. Focus on Zora and your brother, and we'll get through this."

"I will. So you are really good with spells?"

"Aye. You don't see very many rough-handed orcs doing very much spell casting. My deceptions served us well. If the Scourge suspected I was a spell caster, they would have gagged me, and we would have been part of the earth now. Instead, they overlooked me. Took me for another dumb brute." He winked at Grey Cloak and flipped his long blond hair. "My rugged good looks have bailed Rhonna and me out more than a time or two. I knit my brow like this"—he made a mean face—"and the fools don't expect any different."

"A clever disguise."

"I'm hard on the outside and warm and squishy within.

Like a scallop but not as delicious." Lythlenion nudged Grey Cloak. "Don't tell anyone, though."

"I won't."

Later in the day, the cloudy skies brought a hard rain. Tanlin was still coughing. With stinging raindrops hitting their faces, they followed the road north toward the Dark Ridges. The smaller hills that led to the base of the high mountains were rocky and rutted. The muddy road slowed them. Evening began to set in, and the skies became purple and black.

Rhonna stormed ahead, leading them through the rutted road and ignoring the rolling thunder and flashes of lightning.

Tanlin caught up to her and said, "We need to rest."

"No, I don't," she said.

"I need to rest!" Tanlin shouted.

Rhonna grunted and searched the hills. The strange valley had many overlooks, pockets, and dips. She pointed. "There."

Without question, Grey Cloak and the others followed Rhonna to a rocky pocket that was shielded from the rain. They didn't have any tents, pots, or pans. They were roughing it and huddled underneath the overhanging rocks with water pouring down all around them.

Grey Cloak covered up in his cloak the same as everyone else. The thunder sounded like an angry monster in the heavens. The lightning stopped, and without a fire, they were surrounded by the Cimmerian night.

Suddenly, the chill air in front of Grey Cloak washed warm over his face. He nudged Lythlenion, who was huddled beside him. "Did you cast a spell?" he asked.

"No," Lythlenion said. He sniffed the air. "It smells like something is burning."

"Whatever it is, I like it," Tanlin added.

Out of nowhere, lightning lit up the sky like day. Tanlin let out a horrified scream. They were face-to-face with a huge dragon.

EPILOGUE

The dragon pushed Grey Cloak into the rock wall with his nose. His nostrils flared, and his loud sniff sucked Grey Cloak's long hair away from his face.

Tanlin trembled like a leaf and cowered inside his cloak. Rhonna's and Lythlenion's faces were pale.

Grey Cloak swallowed the lump that had built in his throat while his heart beat like a jackrabbit's. He turned his head and eyeballed the dragon's face, which was twice as tall as him. In the dark, he could only make out the silhouette of the dragon's shape, but the glow in the dragon's eyes brought forth illumination.

The dragon spoke. "This is the one," he said in a resonating voice, letting out a steamy breath.

Great warmth washed over them, drying their clothing in an instant.

"I don't want to be burned alive again!" Tanlin cried.

Grey Cloak recognized the dragon's voice, or at least he thought he did, and said, "Cinder?"

"You have a good memory," Anya said. She appeared beside Grey Cloak and held a dagger at his neck.

"How did you do that, Anya?" he said.

"You were more focused on the dragon than me," she said. "Cinder, give us some shelter, please."

Tanlin continued to shake like a leaf and asked with his teeth chattering, "What's going on?"

Cinder unfolded his great wings and stretched them out over the pocket of rocks. The move enclosed them all and shielded them from the rain.

"How about a little fire?" Anya asked. She lowered her dagger from Grey Cloak's neck.

Cinder spit on the ground. An instant campfire started.

The warm light illuminated the makeshift cave, giving everyone a view of everyone else.

Anya took off her open-faced dragon helm. Her damp auburn hair half covered her beautiful face. She stood tall in her plate-mail armor, which didn't make the slightest sound when she moved. She swiped her hair away from her eyes, twisted it in her hand, and rung it out. "I don't make it a habit to fly in the rain. Especially a cold rain." She walked up to Cinder and patted the horn on his nose and warmed her hands on the fire. "Nor do I care to be so far north, either."

"What are you doing here?" Grey Cloak asked.

"Looking for you, Grey Garment." Her gaze fell on Tanlin and Rhonna, then she kept it fixed on the wide-eyed Lythlenion. "Where is your other blond friend?"

"The Doom Riders took him to Dark Mountain."

Anya's jaw tightened, and she clenched her mailed fist. "*What?*"

"We are going to rescue him," Grey Cloak said. "Him and Zora."

"Who is Zora?"

"Another one of our companions. The Scourge kidnapped her," he said. "We are tracking them." He moved closer to her. "Again, why are you here?"

"I've been ordered to take you and Dyphestive with me," she said.

"Why?"

"Because Black Frost wants you both, obviously. You are naturals like me." She paced in front of the fire and patted the pommel of her sword. "Where is the wizard, Dalsay? He should have been protecting you."

Tanlin spoke up. "Drysis and the Doom Riders killed him." He managed to stand but kept his fearful eyes on Cinder. "Are you really Anya the Sky Rider?"

"I am, and who are you?"

He bowed. "Tanlin, a servant of the Wind. I traveled with Dalsay, serving your cause, for over a decade." He motioned to the other two. "This is Rhonna and Lythlenion. These dire circumstances brought us all together."

"Well met," Anya said with a nod.

Tanlin stretched out a shaky hand toward Cinder and politely asked, "May I touch you?"

Cinder's nostrils crinkled, and he sniffed. "I'll allow it."

"Thank you. I've never seen a dragon so large and magnificent." Tanlin ran his hands over Cinder's face. "You are so warm."

"That's because I'm full of fire," Cinder said.

"Don't flatter him. His head is big enough as it is," Anya said. "Go ahead, Rhonna and Lythlenion. Pet him. He doesn't mind unless you are evil, and if you were, you would be dead by now." She hooked Grey Cloak's arm and pulled him away. "We must talk."

"My ears are yours."

"You are coming with me so that you will be safe."

"No, I'm not. I'm going to rescue Zora and Dyphestive."

"Are you mad? Do you really think that you can sneak into Dark Mountain and sneak him out? Black Frost will be expecting that."

"They think I'm dead."

She lifted an eyebrow. "You are certain?"

He nodded.

"Regardless, you are coming with me. It's imperative."

He crossed his arms and said, "I'm not abandoning my

friends. I got them into this, and I'll get them out. Besides, who are you to tell me what to do?"

Anya fastened her grip around his cloak collar and lifted him to his toes. "You listen to me. I risked a great deal coming this far north after you. If Black Frost's forces sniff us out, we will all be dead. Going to Dark Mountain is suicide." She tipped her head at his friends. "And your companions, overmatched." She let go and straightened his ruffled cloak. "I'm sorry to be gruff, but the longer I stay in these ridges, the more likely we'll be caught. We need to move in the cover of rain and darkness."

"Listen, Anya, I appreciate what you are saying, even though I don't completely understand it. Whether I'm a natural or not, it's still my life, and I'll do as I wish."

"I see," she said with a nod. "Well then, if your mind is made up, then I too can respect that." She picked up her helmet and put it on. "Cinder, we are leaving."

"But I was just getting to know these fellas. I like them," Cinder replied. "Nice meeting all of you."

"Yes, you too," Tanlin said like a giddy child.

Cinder closed his wings. The rain poured down, but it didn't drown out the fire.

"Nice meeting all of you," Anya said with a frown. She climbed up Cinder's front foot and into the saddle. Lightning flashed behind them. The hard rain ran down her armor. Her voice carried when she spoke. "Grey Cloak, are you certain that you won't come?"

He noticed all of his friends staring at him and said, "Positive."

"I thought so," Anya replied. "Cinder, take him!"

Cinder's massive foot locked around Grey Cloak's body. The dragon's wings pounded the air, and he launched himself skyward.

Grey Cloak cried, "No! What are you doing?" His arms were pinned to his sides, the dragon's foot trapping him like a huge vise. The ground fell away from him, and the shocked faces of his friends shrank. The dragon fire went out, leaving what was left of Talon alone and in the blackness.

WILL Grey Cloak find a way to escape in time to help his friends?

Can Talon carry on without their leader?

How will Dyphestive survive in clutches of the dreaded Dark Mountain?

What about the mysterious Figurine of Heroes?

Keep turning the pages and learn more.

PLEASE LEAVE a review for Black Frost Book #2 by clicking this link.

READ ON IN DRAGON WARS: Sky Rider - Book 3.
On sale now at Amazon: LINK.

Did you sign up to my newsletter and download a copy of the FREE Dragon Wars Prequel? Sign up here and get 3 FREE books: WWW.DRAGONWARSBOOKS.COM

TEACHERS AND STUDENTS, if you would like to order paperback copies for you library or classroom, email craig@thedarkslayer.com to receive a special discount.

SCROLL ON DOWN if you want to learn more about the mysterious Figurine of Heroes and the strange characters that is summons. It's in the Afterword. And don't forget to grab some cool SWAG! Grab some Dragon Wars Armor below.

GEAR UP in this Dragon Wars body armor enchanted with a +2 Coolness factor/+4 at Gaming Conventions. Sizes range from halfling (Small) to Ogre (XXL). LINK Scroll down for image. www.sociey6.com

Now, about that Figurine of Heroes...

(See next page)

AFTERWORD

The Figurine of Heroes

I hope you are enjoying this series as much as I enjoy writing it. Now that you are two books deep in what is going to be a long series, I thought I would shed some light on things. Mainly, the artifact called the Figurine of Heroes/Horrors. Dalsay used the figurine at the end of Book 1, and we kicked off with it at the beginning of Book 2. The heroes summoned from another fantastical dimension are Venir the Darkslayer and his mount, Chongo, a giant-sized dwarven setter from the world of Bish. You can read more about these heroes from bestselling series:

The Darkslayer: Wrath of the Royals – Book 1 or

The Darkslayer Omnibus (a complete collection of series 1).

Also, Browning and Tanlin mentioned another evil

creature that Dalsay summoned with the figurine. This is Eep the Imp, also an enemy of the Darkslayer.

Interestingly enough, Grey Cloak uses the figurine and brings forth a part-elven wizard, Bayzog. Bayzog's origins are from my Chronicles of Dragon series. You can find him in:

The Hero, the Sword, and the Dragons – Book 1 or

The Chronicles of Dragon Collection (all ten books in the series)

For those of you who have read my books, I hope you enjoy the appearance of some old friends and enemies. And for those of you who are new to my works, I hope you have time to explore more about them. As I've said before, all of my worlds tie together in one way or another. Many more surprises to come. I hope you enjoy.

Ride the Sky,

Craig

ABOUT THE AUTHOR

Craig Halloran resides with his family outside his hometown of Charleston, West Virginia. When he isn't entertaining mankind, he is seeking adventure, working out, or watching sports. To learn more about him, go to www.dragonwarsbooks.com

*Check me out on Bookbub and follow: HalloranOn-BookBub

*I'd love it if you would subscribe to my mailing list: www.craighalloran.com

*On Facebook, you can find me at The Darkslayer Report or Craig Halloran.

*Twitter, Twitter, Twitter. I am there too: www.twitter.com/CraigHalloran

*And of course, you can always email me at craig@thedark-slayer.com

ALSO BY CRAIG HALLORAN

<u>Check out all my great stories...</u>

<u>Free Books</u>

The Darkslayer: Brutal Beginnings

Nath Dragon—Quest for the Thunderstone

<u>The Chronicles of Dragon Series I (10-book series)</u>

The Hero, the Sword and the Dragons (Book 1)

Dragon Bones and Tombstones (Book 2)

Terror at the Temple (Book 3)

Clutch of the Cleric (Book 4)

Hunt for the Hero (Book 5)

Siege at the Settlements (Book 6)

Strife in the Sky (Book 7)

Fight and the Fury (Book 8)

War in the Winds (Book 9)

Finale (Book 10)

Box Set 1-5

Box Set 6-10

Collector's Edition 1-10

Tail of the Dragon, The Chronicles of Dragon, Series 2 (10-book series)

Tail of the Dragon #1

Claws of the Dragon #2

Battle of the Dragon #3

Eyes of the Dragon #4

Flight of the Dragon #5

Trial of the Dragon #6

Judgment of the Dragon #7

Wrath of the Dragon #8

Power of the Dragon #9

Hour of the Dragon #10

Box Set 1-5

Box Set 6-10

Collector's Edition 1-10

The Odyssey of Nath Dragon Series (New Series) (Prequel to Chronicles of Dragon)

Exiled

Enslaved

Deadly

Hunted

Strife

<u>**The Darkslayer Series 1 (6-book series)**</u>

Wrath of the Royals (Book 1)

Blades in the Night (Book 2)

Underling Revenge (Book 3)

Danger and the Druid (Book 4)

Outrage in the Outlands (Book 5)

Chaos at the Castle (Book 6)

Box Set 1-3

Box Set 4-6

Omnibus 1-6

<u>**The Darkslayer: Bish and Bone, Series 2 (10-book series)**</u>

Bish and Bone (Book 1)

Black Blood (Book 2)

Red Death (Book 3)

Lethal Liaisons (Book 4)

Torment and Terror (Book 5)

Brigands and Badlands (Book 6)

War in the Wasteland (Book 7)

Slaughter in the Streets (Book 8)

Hunt of the Beast (Book 9)

The Battle for Bone (Book 10)

Box Set 1-5

Box Set 6-10

Bish and Bone Omnibus (Books 1-10)

CLASH OF HEROES: Nath Dragon meets The Darkslayer mini series

Book 1

Book 2

Book 3

The Henchmen Chronicles

The King's Henchmen

The King's Assassin

The King's Prisoner

The King's Conjurer

The King's Enemies

The King's Spies

The Gamma Earth Cycle

Escape from the Dominion

Flight from the Dominion

Prison of the Dominion

The Supernatural Bounty Hunter Files (10-book series)

Smoke Rising: Book 1

I Smell Smoke: Book 2

Where There's Smoke: Book 3

Smoke on the Water: Book 4

Smoke and Mirrors: Book 5

Up in Smoke: Book 6

Smoke Signals: Book 7

Holy Smoke: Book 8

Smoke Happens: Book 9

Smoke Out: Book 10

Box Set 1-5

Box Set 6-10

Collector's Edition 1-10

Zombie Impact Series

Zombie Day Care: Book 1

Zombie Rehab: Book 2

Zombie Warfare: Book 3

Box Set: Books 1-3

OTHER WORKS & NOVELLAS

The Red Citadel and the Sorcerer's Power